BRAZIL

BRAZIL

Evelyn Bender

CHELSEA HOUSE PUBLISHERS
New York   Philadelphia

COVER: Brightly colored homes enliven a rural Brazilian community.

Chelsea House Publishers

Editor-in-Chief: Nancy Toff
Executive Editor: Remmel T. Nunn
Managing Editor: Karyn Gullen Browne
Copy Chief: Juliann Barbato
Picture Editor: Adrian G. Allen
Art Director: Maria Epes
Manufacturing Manager: Gerald Levine
Systems Manager: Rachel Vigier

Places and Peoples of the World

Editorial Director: Rebecca Stefoff

Staff for BRAZIL
Associate Editor: Kevin Bourke
Copy Editor: Brian Sookram
Deputy Copy Chief: Mark Rifkin
Editorial Assistant: Marie Claire Cebrián
Picture Researcher: Joan Kathryn Beard
Assistant Art Director: Loraine Machlin
Designer: Donna Sinisgalli
Production Manager: Joseph Romano

DF

3   5   7   9   8   6   4

Library of Congress Cataloging-in-Publication Data
Bender, Evelyn.
Brazil / Evelyn Bender.
p. cm.—(Places and peoples of the world)
Summary: Surveys the history, topography, people, and culture of Brazil,
with emphasis on its current economy, industry, and place in the political world.
1. Brazil—Juvenile literature. [1. Brazil.] I. Title. II. Series.
F2508.5.B46 1990 89-28262
981—dc20 CIP AC
ISBN 0-7910-1108-9

CONTENTS

Map	6
Facts at a Glance	9
History at a Glance	11
Chapter 1 Brazil and the World	15
Chapter 2 Geography	21
Chapter 3 History	37
Chapter 4 People	51
Color Section Scenes of Brazil	57
Chapter 5 Government and Social Services	73
Chapter 6 Economy, Transportation, and Communication	83
Chapter 7 Arts and Culture	93
Chapter 8 The Future of Brazil	103
Glossary	107
Index	109

HIGHLANDS

AMAPÁ

River

Belém

Manaus

PARÁ

MARANHÃO

Fortaleza

CEARÁ

RIO GRANDE
DO NORTE

FERNANDO
DE NORONHA

PIAUÍ

PARAÍBA

PERNAMBUCO

Recife

São Francisco River

ALAGOAS

SERGIPE

Salvador

BAHIA

GOIÁS

MATO GROSSO

Brasília
★

FEDERAL
DISTRICT

PANTANAL

MINAS GERAIS

Belo
Horizonte

ESPÍRITO
SANTO

SÃO PAULO

Volta
Redonda

RIO DE JANEIRO

São Paulo

Rio de Janeiro

PARANÁ

SANTA CATARINA

Paraguay-Paraná River

RIO GRANDE
DO SUL

FACTS AT A GLANCE

Land and People

Name	Federative Republic of Brazil (República Federativa do Brasil)
Short Form	Brazil
Area	3,286,478 square miles (8,511,965 square kilometers)
Highest Point	Pico da Neblina, 9,888 feet (2,996 meters)
Greatest Length	2,684 miles (4,294 kilometers)
Greatest Width	2,689 miles (4,302 kilometers)
Major River Systems	Amazon, Paraguay-Paraná-Plata river system, São Francisco
Largest Waterfalls	Iguaçú Falls, Paul Afonso Falls
Capital	Brasília (population 1,577,000)
Other Major Urban Centers	São Paulo (population 15,000,000), Rio de Janeiro (population 10,000,000)
Population of Brazil	144,925,000
Infant Mortality Rate	70 per 1,000 live births

Average Life Expectancy	Women, 66 years; men, 61 years
Official Language	Portuguese
Literacy Rate	Official estimates, 75 percent adult literacy
Ethnic Groups	White, 53 percent; mixed, 34 percent; black, 11 percent; Indians, Asians, and others, 2 percent
Religions	Roman Catholic, 90 percent (including 30 percent African-Brazilian spiritist religions); Buddhists, Protestants , and Jews, 10 percent

Economy

Chief Exports	Coffee, soybeans, oranges, orange juice, sugar, cocoa, iron ore, iron and steel, military equipment, vehicles, hats, shoes
Chief Imports	Oil, chemicals, fertilizers, wheat, machinery
Chief Agricultural Products	Coffee, cotton, corn, beans, rice, cassava, wheat, potatoes, soybeans, sugar, cocoa, oranges, tobacco, bananas, peanuts, rubber
Tourism	About 2 million people visit Brazil every year
Industries	Transportation, communication, and military equipment, oil and fuel products, iron ore, precious metals and gemstones
Average Annual Income	Equal to U.S. $2,370 (1989)

Government

Form of Government	Constitutional republic
Formal Head of State	President
Head of Government	President, elected for a five-year term
Legislature	Two-chambered congress with Senate and Chamber of Deputies
Local Government	23 states, three territories, and the federal district (including Brasília, the capital)

HISTORY AT A GLANCE

before 1500   Native Americans, perhaps 4,000,000 in number, with various languages, customs, and cultures live in the area of present-day Brazil.

1418   Prince Henry the Navigator builds an observatory and a school for explorers in Portugal. Voyages financed and encouraged by Henry expand Portuguese trade in gold and slaves from Africa.

1494   The Treaty of Tordesillas divides South America between Spain and Portugal along a north-south line. Brazil is on the Portuguese side.

1500   Pedro Álvares Cabral lands in Brazil and claims it for Portugal.

1532   The first permanent settlement, São Vicente, is founded on the southern coast of Brazil.

1574   The Jesuit religious order is given control of Indian villages.

1580–1640   Portugal and Spain are united under one king (Philip II of Spain).

1624   The Dutch occupy parts of northeast Brazil and begin to develop government and industry.

1654	The Dutch are driven out of the country. A Brazilian national identity begins to develop.
1693	Gold is discovered in the Minas Gerais region. Mining towns spring up during a gold rush.
1694	Palmares, an independent territory established by escaped slaves, is overcome by Portuguese forces.
1720	Diamonds are discovered in Minas Gerais. The town of Diamantina is founded.
1759	Having become too powerful, the Jesuits are expelled from Brazil.
1789	Tiradentes (Joaquim José da Silva Xavier) leads an unsuccessful movement for independence from Portugal.
1808	Dom John of Portugal (later King John VI) flees to Brazil from Napoleon's troops. His stay in Brazil stimulates the economy and increases trade.
1822	Dom Pedro declares Brazil independent on September 7 and becomes Emperor Pedro I of Brazil.
1840	Pedro II, at 14 years old, becomes emperor. Brazil prospers under his governance.
1888	Slavery is abolished in Brazil; more than 700,000 slaves are set free.
1889	The government becomes a federal republic. Dom Pedro II and his family leave Brazil.
1917	Brazil declares war on Germany in World War I.
1930	Getúlio Vargas leads a rebellion, with the backing of the military, and becomes president.
1942	Brazil declares war against Germany and Italy in World War II.
1954	After agreeing to resign from office, Vargas commits suicide.

1955   Juscelino Kubitschek de Oliveira is elected president.

1960   The capital is moved from Rio de Janeiro to a newly constructed city in the interior, Brasília.

1964   The military seizes control of the government.

1985   The congress chooses Tancredo de Almeida Neves to be president, but Neves dies before taking office. Vice-president José Sarney becomes president.

1988   A new constitution, strengthening some civil rights and environmental laws, is adopted.

1989   Fernando Collor de Mello is elected president.

With its history everywhere in evidence, Brazil faces new challenges, particularly with its growing numbers of poor. In the northeastern city of Salvador, this man sits outside an old colonial building that was built and later abandoned by the Portuguese.

1

Brazil and the World

Brazil is a vast land, the fifth-largest country in the world. It is a country of contrasts and extremes. Its people include tribal Indians as well as sophisticated city dwellers. Its geography features mountain peaks, grassy plains, lush tropical rain forests, beautiful beaches, and several of the world's largest cities. Its urban centers are a mixture of poverty-stricken slums and luxurious apartment houses.

Brazil is the only Portuguese-speaking country in South America. Its customs and traditions differ from those of its Spanish-speaking neighbors. Although the Portuguese influence has been strong in Brazil, however, the Native American Indian peoples who lived there before the arrival of the Europeans and the Africans who were brought as slaves have added their own customs and languages to the Brazilian way of life. Brazil is unique because of this blending.

One example of cultural blending is found in Brazilian religious practice. Most Brazilians are Roman Catholics; Catholic religious festivals and churches are part of the fabric of life. But many Brazilians—including many of the country's Catholics—also participate in African-Brazilian spiritist ceremonies, which combine Catholic saints with African and Indian customs.

Brazilians are very proud of their peaceful history. Although Brazil was a colony of Portugal, it did not have to fight a bitter war for independence, as did many other former colonies. Nor has Brazil been involved in a major local war or a bloody revolution. Even the issue of slavery was settled without violence. However, some of Brazil's governments have been repressive, and some of its leaders have permitted the violation of individual human rights and the censorship of information. After years of military rule, Brazil moved toward a more democratic form of government during the 1980s. A new constitution was adopted in 1988. Among its new features are social services, rights for laborers and women, and benefits for the poor. The first free election for president is scheduled for December 1989.

Brazil contains two of the world's largest cities. They are São Paulo and Rio de Janeiro, the country's two major cities, and they are very different in character. Many world travelers call Rio the loveliest city on earth. It is set on a large blue-water bay, surrounded by mountains and made beautiful by beaches, palm trees, and tropical flowers, birds, and butterflies. Music and art flourish in Rio. Towering over the city, a well-known statue of Christ the Redeemer welcomes strangers and comforts residents. São Paulo is the largest city in South America. It is the business and industrial center of Brazil, similar to New York City in the United States. São Paulo is also the fastest-growing, wealthiest area of Brazil. Brazilians are proud of this city and regard it as a symbol of what Brazil can achieve in the future.

Yet Brazil's cities have many problems. The most urgent of these is poverty. Millions of impoverished people live in the *favelas*, as Brazil's slums are called; many of these destitute people are abandoned or orphaned children. Although the new constitution has formally increased the government's commitment to improving the life of the poor, it is unlikely that social services can meet the need because of the shaky state of the Brazilian economy.

During the 1980s, people around the world became concerned with the fate of the Brazilian rain forests. These forests, some of which are still untouched by the modern world, are part of Brazil's natural resources; they include enormous river systems and hundreds of species of plants and animals found nowhere else in the world. In addition, deposits of iron ore, gold, and other minerals in the rain-forest region have not yet been tapped. Developers, who feel that the land should be farmed or industrialized, are struggling with environmentalists, who believe that at least some of it should be preserved. The developers have proved to be the stronger force, and the rain forest is rapidly being cleared by fire and ax, although scientists are becoming increasingly worried that the loss of so many millions of acres of trees will have a destructive effect on the world's atmosphere.

Brazil is proud of its diverse cultures. These women, from the state of Bahia in eastern Brazil, celebrate the first night of Carnaval in the city of Rio de Janeiro with a traditional samba dance and elaborate costumes.

This irrigation trench is part of a large-scale water management system in the São Francisco River Basin. It is one of many projects designed to help Brazil become more self-sufficient.

The struggle over the fate of the rain forest concerns not only the large commercial developers and the environmentalists but also thousands of landless peasants who are desperately eager to own a plot of land. Plans for redistributing undeveloped land to peasant families have been discussed for years. From time to time, disputes over land have become violent, as landless peasant farmers, environmentalists, and Catholic social activists have clashed with private armies employed by wealthy landowners and developers. Since 1985, about 250 people have died each year in the struggle over ownership of land in the large rain-forest region known as Amazonia, in northern Brazil. The struggle is centered in the remote northwestern states of Amazonas, Rondônia, and Acre.

Since World War II, Brazil has developed its manufacturing, mining, and other commercial activities to become the eighth-largest industrial nation in the world. It produces cars, ships, airplanes, electrical appliances, and—in its most recently developed industry—arms and military equipment. It also supplies many agricultural products to the world, including coffee, soybeans, oranges, orange juice, sugar, cocoa, tobacco, poultry, and livestock. Brazil places great importance on becoming self-sufficient—that is, able to produce all of the materials and products its people need. One step toward self-sufficiency has been the development of ethanol, a mixture of alcohol and gasoline that has helped Brazil reduce its dependence on oil imported from foreign nations, although much oil must still be imported. Brazil is also developing nuclear plants to supply power for commercial and home use.

Brazil is a natural leader in South America because it is the largest country on the continent, because it has a correspondingly large population of 144,925,000, and because of its extensive resources. Although Brazil has long been allied with the United States, it is now seeking a more independent stance in international politics. In recent years, Brazil has forged closer ties with African, Asian, Arab, and European countries, as well as with the Soviet Union. In terms of international affairs, Brazil is sometimes seen as the leader of the world's developing nations, most of which are located in Africa, Asia, and South America. It is probable that leadership among these Third World countries will continue to be one of Brazil's roles in the future.

The Iguaçú Falls, located at the point where Brazil, Paraguay, and Argentina meet, is more than two miles (3.2 kilometers) wide and averages 200 feet (61 meters) in height. The Iguaçú River, which feeds into the falls, flows west from the state of Paraná.

2

Geography

Brazil is the fifth-largest country in the world, after the Soviet Union, Canada, the People's Republic of China, and the United States. It is the largest country in South America—in fact, Brazil occupies about half of that continent. Brazil shares boundaries with every other South American nation except Ecuador and Chile. Its neighbors to the north are French Guiana, Suriname, Guyana, and Venezuela; to the northwest, Colombia; to the west, Peru and Bolivia; to the southwest, Paraguay and Argentina; and to the south, Uruguay. On the northeast, east, and southeast, Brazil's shores are washed by the Atlantic Ocean.

Shaped roughly like a triangle balanced on its tip, Brazil stretches 2,684 miles (4,294 kilometers) from north to south and 2,689 miles (4,302 kilometers) from east to west. Its area is 3,286,478 square miles (8,511,965 square kilometers)—just slightly larger than the area of the United States without Alaska and Hawaii. Brazil's Atlantic shoreline is 4,600 miles (7,360 kilometers) long.

Although it has no towering mountain ranges, Brazil consists of highlands and lowlands. The large basin of the Amazon River in the north is low; the western part of the country is also low-lying and rather flat. But in the far north, beyond the Amazon Basin, a range of low but rugged mountains called the Guiana Highlands straddles Brazil's border with Colombia, Venezuela, and other nations. Brazil's highest point is here, right on the Venezuelan border. It is called Pico da Neblina, which means "hazy peak," and it is 9,888 feet (2,996 meters) high. South of the Amazon Basin, the whole eastern part of the country is called the Brazilian Highlands. It is a region of hills and plateaus between 1,000 and 3,000 feet (300 and 910 meters) above sea level. Along much of the Atlantic coast, this highland drops steeply to the sea in a cliff called the Great Escarpment. In a few places, however, there is a narrow strip of coastal lowland between the highland and the sea.

Geographers usually divide Brazil into five main regions based on differences in climate and land features. These geographic regions are the Amazon, the Northeast, the West Central, the Southeast, and the South.

The Amazon Region

The Amazon region, or Amazonia, in the north, covers two-fifths of the country but is home to only seven percent of the population. This region is dominated by the tropical rain forest, the world's largest—at 2.8 million square miles (7.35 million square kilometers) in area, the rain forest is nearly the size of Australia. The warm temperatures and abundant rainfall of the forest are so favorable to life that animals and plants flourish in every available spot. The 80 °F (27 °C) temperature seems higher because of the humidity from the 87-inch (221-centimeter) annual rainfall.

About half of all the kinds of living things in the world—5 million species or separate types—can be found in the Amazon. More than 3,000 separate types of plants have been identified in a single square mile (2.6 square kilometers). Among the trees are myrtles, laurels, palms, Brazil nuts, brazilwood, mahogany, wild-rubber trees, kapok trees, rosewood, and fig trees. Some grow to heights of 200 feet (60 meters) in their search for sunlight. They provide

Many Brazilians believe that land development—building roads, bridges, and houses—is needed to sustain the country's growing population and to improve its economy. Others fear that development, by destroying the rain forests, may damage the world environment.

support for lianas, or vines, as well as for orchids, ferns, and cacti that grow in crevices in the tree bark. Tropical fruits such as papayas, guavas, and plantains (similar to bananas) are food sources for monkeys, birds, and fruit bats, as well as for the people of the region. Many familiar North American and European house plants—for example, philodendrons—grow wild in the rain forest. One section of the forest is called the canopy. This is the dense layer of upper branches and leaves, high above the forest floor. More animals, birds, and insects live in this dark and humid rooftop world than in any other part of the rain forest.

Plants absorb carbon dioxide from the atmosphere and release oxygen into the air; the plant life of the Amazon provides about one-third of the world's oxygen, which is necessary for animal life.

This is one of the reasons why scientists are so concerned about the loss of millions of acres of the rain forest to development. No one is certain of the effect that this loss will have on the planet's atmosphere, but it appears that far-reaching global changes—such as the phenomenon called global warming, which involves an increase of carbon dioxide in the atmosphere and gradually rising temperatures all over the world—can be linked to the destruction of forest lands.

The encroachment of developers into the rain forest also threatens the region's wildlife. Brazil's forest creatures include several

The two-toed sloth is one of the thousands of animal species that live in the rain forests of the Amazon.

members of the cat family: jaguars, pumas, ocelots, and spotted leopards. Admired as adroit hunters by the Indians, jaguars are the subject of many native folktales. When settlement takes over the forest, jaguars are sometimes killed because of their threat to cattle and people, and all the Brazilian wild cats have been hunted for their spotted coats. Other rain forest creatures include monkeys, deer, anteaters, bush dogs, sloths (shaggy mammals that hang from tree limbs by their powerful claws), tapirs (large grazing animals with long snouts), peccaries (wild pigs), capybaras (the world's largest rodents), and armadillos. Bats are numerous; most feed on fruit or insects, but some—the so-called vampire bats—feed on blood, which they lap from the shallow bites they inflict on livestock or sleeping people.

There are 1,800 species of birds in the Amazon. Many of them are brightly colored parrots, macaws, and toucans. The world's largest eagle, the harpy eagle, is also found there, as are ducks, ibis, woodpeckers, and hummingbirds. Reptiles of the region include several deadly snake species: the bushmaster, the fer-de-lance, and the giant anaconda, which can reach lengths of 30 feet (10 meters). One-third of the world's million species of insects live in the Amazon. Among them are killer bees, army ants, and hundreds of varieties of large, jewel-colored butterflies, which are prized by collectors and even used in jewelry.

The Amazon River rises in the Andes Mountains of Peru and flows across the breadth of Brazil from west to east to empty into the Atlantic Ocean. It is the major geographic feature of northern Brazil—indeed, it is one of the principal land features of the South American continent. The Amazon is the world's second-longest river, with a total length of 3,900 miles (6,240 kilometers), most of which lies within Brazil's borders. The Nile River in Africa is longer, but the Amazon carries more water. It discharges one-fifth of all the water that flows into the oceans from the world's rivers. At its mouth near the city of Belém, the Amazon is 90 miles (140 kilometers) wide, and upstream its width varies from 5 to 40 miles (8 to 64 kilometers). Of the more than 500 rivers that flow into the Amazon, 15 are longer than 1,000 miles (1,600 kilometers). Large, oceangoing ships can sail as far upriver as the city of Manaus, more than 1,000 miles (1,600 kilometers) from the sea.

Among the 2,500 kinds of fish that are native to the Amazon River are the piranhas, known as tiger fish or cannibal fish, which have very strong jaws and razor-sharp teeth. A person or animal that falls into piranha-infested waters may be stripped down to a skeleton in a few minutes. Piranhas are fairly small, and each can take only a small bite at a time, but these fish overpower their prey by attacking swiftly and in the hundreds. Piranha jaws have been used as efficient cutting devices by the Indians.

Other dangerous fish species include the electric eel, the stingray, and the giant catfish. One fish that is used for food is the pirarucu, or giant redfish. This is the world's largest freshwater fish. It has been known to reach a length of 15 feet (5 meters) and a weight of 600 pounds (270 kilograms). Many of the small tropical fish that live in aquariums all over the world also come from the Amazon. The giant river otter, a playful, social mammal about six feet (two meters) long, is another water dweller, although it is becoming rare. Frogs, toads, turtles, crocodiles, and several species of caimans (similar to alligators) abound.

Although many environmentalists are opposed to the development of industry in the Amazon, one industry is well suited to preserving the rain forest. That industy is rubber tapping, which was first practiced by the Indians. Latex, the milk of the rubber tree, is drained and processed to make tires and other products; in this industry, the rubber trees are used, but not destroyed. The *seringueros*, as the rubber workers are called, have formed a union to oppose the wholesale destruction of the rain forest, but many developers and large landowners have hired private armies to protect their interests. Farmers, soldiers, miners, Indians, and serin-

Early explorers in Brazil astonished the world with tales of the giant anaconda, the world's largest snake.

gueros have died fighting over the land and the forest. This battle seized the world's attention in December 1988, when Francisco "Chico" Mendes, a seringuero of Acre state who had led the rubber workers' movement, was murdered on the doorstep of his home. A rancher and his two sons have been convicted of killing Mendes, and the slain seringuero has become a symbol of the fight to preserve the forest.

The greatest damage to the forest is caused by the slash-and-burn method used for clearing the land. In this method, the trees are cut down, and then the cleared area is burned to destroy the stumps and other vegetation. Unfortunately for the would-be farmers who flock to the Amazon to clear new patches of land, the rain forest soil is poorly suited to agriculture, and an acre that supported rain forest for a thousand years will produce good crops for only two or three years. Nonetheless, about 30,000 square miles (78,600 square kilometers) of rain forest are cleared each year.

A new threat to the Amazon is the discovery of oil in the heart of the rain forest. Brazil is anxious to produce its own petroleum, because it now imports half of the 1.1 million barrels it uses every day. Ecologists, however, are concerned about the danger of pollution from oil spills in the forest or the river and about the destruction involved in the building of pipelines.

The Northeast Region

The northeast region of Brazil covers about one-fifth of the country and houses one-fourth of the population. Conditions there are difficult. Unemployment is high, and there is little industry. The land along the Atlantic coast is fertile and supports crops such as cacao beans, sugarcane, coffee, and tobacco, but the interior of the region has poor soil. Farmers raise cattle and cultivate beans, cassava, corn, and cotton. Much of this farming is at the subsistence level, however—that is, the farmers produce barely enough to feed themselves and their families. Frequent droughts, some lasting two years, have caused desert conditions. Life expectancy in the northeast averages 49 years, much lower than in the rest of the country.

The cities of Fortaleza, Recife, and Salvador are found in the northeast, as is the São Francisco River, which starts near Brasília, deep in the interior, and flows 900 miles (1,500 kilometers) north and then east toward the sea. Its course is broken 190 miles (306 kilometers) from the ocean by the Paul Afonso Falls, a waterfall 275 feet (84 meters) high.

Temperatures in the northeast cover a wide range, particularly in the interior, where thermometers may read anything from 53°F to 107°F (12°C to 42°C). The coast experiences less dramatic changes, with an average temperature of 80°F (27°C). While drought is a severe problem, occasional heavy rains in parts of the interior can cause flooding. Rainfall on the coast averages 65 inches (169 centimeters) a year.

Because the northeast was where the slave ships docked, this region is the most "Africanized." African customs, images, and language have influenced the art, music, religion, and cuisine here more than in other parts of Brazil. The state of Bahia, in particular, has a large proportion of African-Brazilian inhabitants.

The West Central Region

The west central region covers about one-fourth of Brazil and has five percent of its population. Brasília (population 1,577,000), which has been Brazil's capital since 1960, is located in this region. Much of the west central region is occupied by the Pantanal, a lowland

The late Francisco "Chico" Mendes fought to protect the rain forests from land developers. The best known of the hundreds of Brazilians who have been killed in the conflict over the fate of the forests, Mendes has become an international symbol of the struggle in the Amazon Basin.

941223

with swamps, marshes, and many lakes and rivers. Little agriculture is possible in the Pantanal, but cattle are raised in some of its drier patches. An enormous wildlife sanctuary is located in the Pantanal; it is home to many of the species found in the Amazon region, but here these animals live in open woodlands and marshy grasslands instead of in dense jungle. Alligators, armadillos, monkeys, capy-baras, jaguars, and many types of birds and fish are found in the Pantanal.

The annual rainfall in the west central region is 40 inches (102 centimeters). Most of it falls in the rainy season, from October to

On the banks of the Amazon River, near the interior port city of Manaus, the house and farm of a rural family are set in a clearing in the forest.

April. Outside the Pantanal are large cattle ranches, soybean farms, and growing cities and towns. The population of this region is expected to grow as industry is gradually introduced and more areas of the Pantanal are opened to livestock ranching.

The Southeast Region

The southeast has 10 percent of the land and 47 percent of the population. The two largest cities in Brazil are found in this region: Rio de Janeiro and São Paulo. Since the 1940s, country people have been moving to the cities—particularly to these two cities, both of which are surrounded by huge, sprawling suburbs. In 1945, two-thirds of Brazilians lived in rural areas, but by 1980 two-thirds lived in cities. This urban growth occurred because rural people sought the greater job opportunities of the towns, but today not all those who seek urban jobs can find them.

Rio de Janeiro, with a population of 10 million, is second to São Paulo in the number of inhabitants and the size of its businesses and industries but has always been considered the cultural center of the country, with excellent theaters, museums, and libraries. Writers, artists, architects, and musicians participate in the creative life of the city. The city's best-known landmark is Sugarloaf Mountain, a cone-shaped rock 1,300 feet (390 meters) high that stands at the entrance of Rio's harbor. Another spectacular sight is Corcovado Mountain. It is 2,300 feet (700 meters) tall, topped with a statue of Christ the Redeemer that is 124 feet (38 meters) high and weighs 700 tons (777 metric tons); the statue's outstretched arms are 92 feet (28 meters) across. The statue was built in 1931 to commemorate the independence of Brazil.

Rio is a tropical city, but its tropical heat is moderated by the ocean breezes; the areas behind the mountains have higher temperatures. The city's average temperature in the summer is 79 °F (26 °C); in the winter it is 68 °F (20 °C). Because of the warm climate, the beaches are crowded every day of the year. Rainfall averages 44 inches (110 centimeters) a year.

Two structures reflect the interests of the *cariocas*, as the residents of Rio are called. The Sambodromo, with seats for 60,000 people, was erected for spectators of the annual Carnaval parade. The Maracanã Stadium, among the world's largest sport centers, was built for soccer matches and has a capacity of 200,000. The playing ground is surrounded by a deep moat to keep excited fans off the field.

Rio's most serious problem is poverty. Shantytowns and slums, called favelas, have spread to cover many of the hillsides around the city. These are home to several million squatters. Many of them live in crowded shacks made of cardboard or other scrap materials, without such services as water, sewer systems, and electricity. However, not all of the *favelados*, as the residents of these favelas are called, are poor. Some successful people—even middle-class people—live there. The favelas have such organizations as churches, soccer clubs, and samba clubs (sponsors of Carnaval entries). A favela is like a small city in itself. As the favelas have gradually gained a variety of inhabitants and a measure of respectability, some of the houses have been improved and made permanent, but crime and illegal drug traffic continue to flourish.

Another urban problem is homeless children. Approximately 16 million abandoned children roam the streets of Brazil's cities, fending for themselves, often stealing in order to eat. A related problem is the giving away or selling of unwanted babies.

With 15 million people, São Paulo is the largest city in South America and a rival of Mexico City for the title of the largest city in Latin America. It is the business and industrial center of the country, where people are intensely engaged in making money and enjoying the urban pleasures of restaurants, shops, theaters, art galleries, opera, and nightclubs. *Paulistas*, or natives of São Paulo, have long had a reputation for being hardworking, ambitious, clever, and

This community is situated literally on the Solimões River, a tributary of the Amazon River in the northwest. Most Brazilians live within a few miles of a major waterway, leaving the interior sparsely populated.

demanding. Like other cities, however, São Paulo has the usual urban problems of poverty, pollution, and city services that lag behind the needs of the population.

In addition to its outstanding cultural institutions, museums, large zoo, and orchid farm, São Paulo is famous for the Instituto Butantan, a large snake farm, which produces snakebite serum for use around the world. Visitors can watch experts "milk" venom from the fangs of poisonous snakes. In addition to its collection of 70,000 snakes, the institute houses other poisonous creatures: reptiles, scorpions, spiders, and insects.

São Paulo, South America's leading business and financial center, is home to 15 million people, making it the second largest city in the Western Hemisphere (after Mexico City). At its current rate of growth, by the year 2000 São Paulo could become the most heavily populated city in the world.

Although São Paulo is located in the tropics, its high elevation and cloud cover give it a temperate climate, with an average temperature of 67 °F (19 °C). It is not a coastal city; its port is Santos, 33 miles (53 kilometers) to the southeast.

The Southern Region

The south accounts for 5 percent of Brazil's area and 16 percent of its population. The climate here is cooler than in the Amazon and the northeast. There are occasional frosts and light snows in the winter months (June to August). The south is the country of the *gauchos*, or cowboys, who work on enormous cattle ranches on the region's sweeping grasslands. The fertile soil of the area also supports large coffee plantations.

The world's largest hydroelectric project is located in this region. It is the Itaipu Dam, which Brazil and Paraguay built together on the Paraná River (part of the Paraguay-Paraná-Plata river system). The dam is 4,900 feet (1,500 meters) high and is located not far from the Iguaçú Falls. Like so much in Brazil, the Iguaçú Falls are magnificent and huge—2 miles (3 kilometers) wide and 237 feet (72 meters) high.

Brazil's vast area includes regions that differ geographically, historically, and culturally. But, although its population of 144,925,000 is larger than that of any other South American country, the inhabitants are not distributed evenly throughout the country. Most Brazilians live within a few hundred miles (or kilometers) of the seacoast. Huge tracts of the interior are almost empty of human life. Attempts have been made to tame, settle, and develop this huge and potentially productive interior, but that goal has not yet been reached. Many Brazilians—and others around the world—now hope that it can be achieved without irreversible damage to Brazil's unique natural heritage, the rain forest.

A Camayura Indian from the Mato Grosso region near the western border plays the pan-pipe. Approximately 100,000 aboriginal Indians live completely outside the sphere of modern industrial Brazil.

3

History

For thousands of years before the coming of Europeans to the Americas, Brazil's Native American peoples lived in settlements along the rivers and on the coast or roamed the interior in hunting bands. Many of these Indians were expert hunters, farmers, and fishermen. Their way of life was tailored to their environment, and they knew much about the habits of animals and the uses of plants. Most of these Indian peoples extracted poisons from various plants and fishes to use on the hunting darts they shot from blowguns; they also obtained drugs for medicinal and magical uses from the forest plants. Some groups of Indians were warlike, conducting raids on other tribes for revenge or to prove their bravery. A few practiced cannibalistic rites, in which human flesh was eaten.

Most Brazilian Indian peoples, however, were cooperative and had a strong belief in sharing. Religious practices, storytelling, and music were important parts of their way of life. But the arrival of the Portuguese in 1500 was to change the life of most of the 4 million Indians who lived in Brazil at that time. Centuries of fighting, repression, and diseases brought by the whites have taken a heavy toll on the Indian population. Some tribes have been completely wiped out. Approximately 100,000 Indians survive today, but their traditional culture is rapidly being changed by contact with the modern world, and some people fear that it may be lost forever.

The Portuguese Explorers and Colonists

In the 16th century, Portugal, which shares the Iberian Peninsula with Spain, was one of the strongest colonial powers in Europe. Its geographic location, at the western edge of Europe and washed by the Atlantic Ocean on two sides, encouraged the development of shipbuilding and sailing. Explorers pushed their way around Africa and across the Indian Ocean to Asia, claiming territory and starting colonies as they went. Portugal's supremacy in seafaring during this era was largely due to Prince Henry the Navigator, who in 1418 had founded a school in southern Portugal for explorers. He encouraged and financed voyages intended to expand the trade in gold and slaves from Africa.

Although a few earlier explorers visited the coast of Brazil and made crude maps of it, credit for beginning European settlement in Brazil has traditionally gone to Pedro Álvares Cabral, who arrived in April 1500 with a fleet of 13 ships and 1,500 men. At the time, Spain and Portugal were competing to claim territories in the Americas. The rivalry between the two was settled by an agreement called the Treaty of Tordesillas, which was proposed by the pope and signed in 1494 (two years after Columbus's first voyage to the New World). The treaty divided the Americas along a line extending north and south 370 leagues (1,110 miles, or 1,787 kilometers) west of the Cape Verde Islands off the African coast. Spain was permitted to claim the lands west of the line, while those east of the line went to Portugal. The treaty line divided Brazil from the rest of South America and gave it to Portugal, and this is why Brazil was colonized by the Portuguese while all the other Latin American nations were colonized by the Spanish. (The name Brazil comes from the brazilwood tree, which yields a dye that was once used for

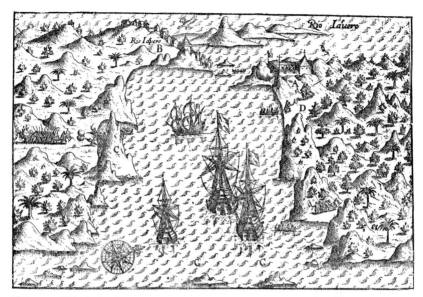

This map of Rio de Janeiro was made in 1599. On the left (at letter C) is Sugarloaf Mountain. At the top (letter B) is the town of Rio de Janeiro. And on the right (letters A and D) are a Portuguese fort and an area for prisoners.

coloring red cloth. Shiploads of this wood were the first profitable commodity to be sent from the colony to Portugal.)

Another expedition left Portugal for the New World in 1501. The pilot was Amerigo Vespucci (the only person for whom two continents have been named: North and South America). As the ship made its way along the Brazilian coast, Vespucci named many of the geographic features after Roman Catholic saints. For example, the São Francisco River was sighted on the day that is dedicated to Saint Francis. (São is Portuguese for "saint.") When the expedition sailed into the huge Guanabara Bay on January 1, 1502, the bay was mistaken for a river and named Rio de Janeiro (River of January). The name has remained for the city that arose there.

For the next 25 years, Portugal was busy with its interests in India and Africa. Eventually, however, settlements were established in Brazil. The first Europeans to live there were *degredados*, Portuguese criminals who were set ashore and left to fend for themselves. Many managed to learn the Indians' languages and customs. Some married Indian women and raised families. Their children of mixed Portuguese and Indian descent were the first generation of a new people, the Brazilians.

Another group of early settlers were *conversos*, or "new Christians"—that is, Jews who had been forced to become Christians by the Catholic church in Europe. Seeking religious freedom, these and practicing Jews fled Spain and Portugal in the late 1400s and early 1500s. Some went directly to Brazil; others went to the Netherlands and then on to the Americas. They became an important force in the sugar industry in Brazil.

In 1532, the first permanent settlement, São Vicente, was founded on the southern coast of Brazil. In order to develop and govern its huge Brazilian territory, Portugal divided the land into 14 captaincies. A captain was appointed to govern each district, develop the land, and collect taxes. This system was formally abolished in 1759. Long before that, however, a centralized system of government started to form in the colony, mainly to supervise land grants. A governor general was appointed in 1549; he was directly responsible to the king of Portugal. Local governing bodies were established, and the coast was fortified. More settlers were attracted to the country. By 1600, there were 57,000 people living in the colony: 25,000 whites, 18,000 Indians, and 14,000 African slaves.

Indians were captured to provide labor for the sugar plantations. They did not prove to be efficient workers, however. Many died of European diseases such as smallpox because they had no immunity to them. Others fought against the Portuguese and were killed. Many of the Indians who became slaves died working in the fields, unable to adjust to a way of life that was completely different from that of the forest.

Enslaving the Indians became illegal in 1570, although the practice continued. The inhabitants of the new town of São Paulo made slave raids. Expeditions called *bandeiras* (flags) were formed to seek out gold and gems as well as to capture slaves. Some of these bandeiras lasted for years and involved whole families. They were also very wide ranging—some went as far as present-day Peru and Colombia. Years later, the raiders, known as *bandeirantes*, were regarded as heroes because they were trailblazers, opening up the western frontiers. Like many heroes of the United States Old West,

The Portuguese made slaves of the Africans they took from the western and southwestern African coasts. In addition, the Portuguese enslaved the native Indian populations, although this practice was officially illegal. When slavery was finally outlawed in 1888, more than 700,000 people were set free.

the bandeirantes combined elements of lawlessness, courage, and adventurousness.

The need for cheap labor stimulated the intercontinental slave trade. African slaves were brought from Dahomey, the Ivory Coast, and the Congo region in western and central Africa. Portuguese sea captains bought slaves from African chiefs in exchange for tobacco, rum, and other goods, then transported them to Brazil and exchanged them for loads of sugar and molasses. Some of the slaves ran away and set up independent territories. The most famous of these settlements was Palmares, where 20,000 escaped slaves lived. Under a leader named Zumbi, they held out against one raid after another until 1694, when they were overcome by a force of paulistas and enslaved once again.

Another historically influential group was the Jesuits, members of the Society of Jesus, a Catholic religious order for men. They sailed to Brazil with the first governor general. In addition to establishing schools, they founded missions in Bahia and São Paulo, where they converted and protected the Indians. In 1574, the Jesuits were given the right to control and protect Indian villages, although Indians could still be captured and enslaved in warfare. Because many colonists objected to the increasing power of the Jesuits, the order was expelled from Brazil in 1759.

Over the years, Portugal had to protect Brazil from other countries' takeover attempts. France tried to start a colony, but was forced out. Beginning in 1624, the Dutch occupied some territory, but they were driven out in 1654. The colonists in Brazil united against the Dutch, and their sense of a Brazilian identity—of being citizens of their own land, separate from Portugal—was strengthened by this experience.

Portugal and Spain were joined under one monarchy from 1580 to 1640, and the two countries' colonies in South America were briefly united. But when Spain and Portugal again became separate in 1640, Portugal began restoring its colonial boundaries in Brazil.

The bandeirantes had pushed the borders of Brazil much farther west than the Treaty of Tordesillas had indicated, but new treaties gave the land to the people who occupied them. Much of the western portion of present-day Brazil was acquired at this time.

Colonial Life

No great cities developed during the early years of the colony. The economy was based on land—on farming, livestock raising, and mining. The two major products were sugar and gold. The sugar plantations were located in the northeast and owned by a few wealthy families, whose way of life was much like that of the plantation owners of the southern United States before the Civil War. Sugar earned huge profits for the landowners and for Portugal, the parent country, for about 200 years.

In 1693, paulistas discovered gold in Minas Gerais, in the southeast region. During the gold rush that followed, new towns sprang up overnight and fortunes were made and lost equally quickly. Around 1720, diamonds were found in the same area. African slaves who had experience in mining taught the Brazilians mining techniques. The town of Diamantina became famous in Europe as the diamond center of the world. While the gold-mining industry lasted for about a century, diamond mining is still going on to this day. The discovery of huge diamond fields in South Africa, however, reduced the importance of Brazil's diamonds. But other precious stones—including amethysts, emeralds, and rubies—are mined in Minas Gerais and contribute a substantial proportion of the world's gems.

Independence

As time went on, some colonists began to desire independence from Portugal. In 1789, a man called Tiradentes led a rebellion against Portugal. (The name, which means "tooth puller," was a nickname for Joaquim José da Silva Xavier, because he was a folk healer who sometimes performed dental extractions.) Tiradentes was arrested and executed, but he became a national hero.

War and upheaval in Europe also affected Brazil's history. Napoleon Bonaparte of France invaded Portugal in 1807, forcing the royal family and about 15,000 Portuguese subjects to flee to Brazil. They arrived in Rio, which was then the capital, in 1808. Prince John, who later became King John VI, remained in Brazil until 1821. During this period, Brazil ended its days as a colony; it became part of a united kingdom with Portugal. Trade and the Brazilian economy flourished.

However, many Brazilians resented King John VI's government because its officials were dishonest and wasteful. In addition, the ideas of revolution and independence were taking hold throughout Latin America. When John returned to Portugal, he left Brazil in the care of his son, Prince Pedro. But the Portuguese parliament feared that Pedro might lead a Brazilian revolution, because he was known to favor independence; the parliament therefore summoned him to Portugal.

Pedro refused to go. Instead, he declared independence for Brazil. On September 7, 1822, on the banks of the Ipiuranga River near São Paulo, Dom Pedro uttered the Grito, or Cry of Ipiuranga: "Independence or death!" He was crowned Emperor Pedro I of Brazil in December 1822. The United States recognized Brazil's independence in 1824; Portugal followed suit in 1825.

Pedro's reign was made difficult by three factors: the problems of establishing a constitutional government, civil war in the provinces, and war with Argentina (in which Brazil lost some territory). He lost popular support. After a military revolt against him, he stepped down from the throne in favor of his five-year-old son, another Pedro. Advisers appointed by Pedro I governed the country for nine years. Then, at the age of 14, in 1840, Pedro II was declared old enough to rule. He matured into a modest, democratic, scholarly man. Tall and full bearded, he had a commanding presence.

Pedro II worked to improve the government and expand the economy. The coffee, cattle, sugar, cotton, and tobacco industries thrived. His rule (1840–89) was a time of peace and prosperity, with development in the arts and sciences. Antislavery sentiment grew strong, especially after the abolition of slavery in the United States, and slavery was finally outlawed in Brazil in 1888; more than 700,000 slaves were set free. At the same time, ideas about democracy became increasingly popular. In 1889, Brazilians revolted against imperial rule. The revolution was bloodless and rather peaceful, but it ended Pedro's reign. He and his family left the country. Brazil became a republic, headed by an elected president.

Dom Pedro II became emperor of Brazil when he was 14 years old. During his reign, he concentrated on developing the economy and encouraging arts and sciences.

Getúlio Vargas made himself dictator in a coup d'état and ran Brazil for a quarter of a century. Eventually his government crumbled under the weight of demands for democratic reforms and its own corruption.

Modern History

Brazil's constitution was modeled on the United States's system of government, with a president, a congress, and basic freedoms for the people. Several presidents with army backgrounds were followed in the mid-1890s by a civilian (nonmilitary) head of government. Progress was made on several fronts: Brazil's economic foundations were strengthened, its cities were enlarged, boundary disputes were settled, treaties were signed with neighboring countries, and the deadly disease yellow fever was wiped out in Rio de Janeiro.

In 1917, after the ship *Paraná* was torpedoed and other Brazilian ships were sunk in World War I sea battles, Brazil declared war on Germany. Brazil supported the United States and its allies in World War I by sending aviators, medical personnel, and ships to the war front. Brazil also contributed food supplies and other resources to the war effort.

The 1920s saw many changes in Brazil. Industries were booming, and a new class of working people arose. Cities were expanding rapidly, and this urban explosion was causing new problems of overpopulation and poverty. Military influence on the government was strong, but antimilitary and communist parties and movements found a growing following. Economic troubles developed when the price of coffee, an important export, dropped and Brazil's earnings fell. Rubber also became less profitable because of the competition from new rubber plantations in Asia. The worldwide economic depression and unemployment of the 1930s affected Brazil and slowed its growth.

In 1930, a provincial governor named Getúlio Vargas led a rebellion with the help of the army and made himself head of the government. He remained in power, a virtual dictator, for most of the next 24 years. Although his regime was at first honest and efficient, it soon became corrupt and repressive.

In 1942, in the middle of World War II, Brazil declared war on Germany and Italy. Brazil was the only South American country to send troops to the battlefields of Italy and Africa. The United States used Brazilian naval and air bases during the war. In addition, Brazil helped defend the South Atlantic against German submarines.

After the war ended in 1945, the Brazilian people demanded democratic reforms. A new constitution was adopted and Vargas was elected president, but he was unable to solve Brazil's growing economic problems. Brazilians began demanding his resignation. In 1954, he agreed to resign, but killed himself with a bullet to the head a few months before he was due to leave office.

Juscelino Kubitschek de Oliveira, who followed Vargas as president, believed in a strong role for the national government. Under his leadership, a new capital, Brasília, was constructed. Located in

In 1985, Tancredo de Almeida Neves was chosen by congress and the military to be president, but he died soon after the election.

the interior of the country to stimulate economic growth there, Brasília is a rarity among cities because it was completely planned before it was built. Oscar Niemeyer and other famous Brazilian architects designed its buildings. Although Brasília remains the national capital, the surge in settlement and development of the area around the city that was expected by government planners has not materialized. The population of the region has increased, and some industries and businesses have sprung up, but this growth has lagged behind the forecasts. Brasília may simply be too far from the coast and from Brazil's other major cities for it to become a hub of commerce, industry, and settlement.

In 1964, the armed forces took over Brazil's government. Under various leaders, military dictatorships controlled the country for the next 21 years. During the 1970s and 1980s, mass demonstrations against government oppression—including a strike by 300,000 metalworkers in São Paulo in 1980 that was quelled by army troops and tanks—brought about a gradual loosening of restrictions. Censorship of the press was ended, and citizens won the right to form as many political parties as they choose (only two had been permitted by the military government before 1979). In January 1985, the military regime bowed to popular pressure and appointed a civilian president, Tancredo de Almeida Neves. Many foreign dignitaries, including U.S. vice-president George Bush, flew to Brasília for Neves's inauguration. The day before the inauguration ceremony, however, Neves became seriously ill with diverticulitis, an intestinal inflammation. He died in April 1985 and José Sarney, the vice-president, became president.

Sarney pledged to restore democracy to Brazil. Changes began in several areas. The government started an agricultural reform program, in which unused land is purchased from rich landowners and given to poor farmers. The Cruzado Plan established a new currency, the cruzado, which replaced the cruzeiro. Labor laws were passed that allowed for collective bargaining (mutual agreements between unions and employers on wages and working conditions). The first unemployment compensation program was set up. A new constitution was adopted in 1988; it strengthened some civil rights and environmental laws.

Fernando Collor de Mello was elected president in December 1989. He has pledged to devote himself to salvaging Brazil's ruined economy. "I want Brazil to be once again a land of opportunity," he declared, "above all, for the younger generation."

A crowd gathers at a religious festival in Juazeiro do Norte in the northeastern state of Ceará. In Brazil, where 90 percent of the population is Roman Catholic, important religious celebrations are also a source of entertainment.

4

People

Three main ethnic groups have shaped the culture and way of life of Brazilians. These are the Native American Indian peoples, the Africans, and the Portuguese.

The native people of Brazil were called Indians by explorers who mistook the Americas for India. Approximately 4 million aborigines, or earliest known inhabitants, lived throughout Brazil in small groups with separate languages and customs; they differed from each other as much as the French, Italians, and Russians differ. Many Indian peoples developed complex cultures and rich mythologies. A great deal of the Indian heritage has become part of Brazilian life, including food, language, art, religious customs, folklore, medicine, and knowledge of the environment.

The future of those Indians who still follow their traditional way of life deep in the forests outside the cash economy of contemporary Brazil is being debated. Several courses of action are possible. The Indians could enter the modern world, either rapidly or at a slow, controlled pace. But some Indians prefer isolation and want to preserve their culture and their traditional way of life—hunting, fishing, and cultivating small plots of crops in the forest. For example, the Kaiapo people, who live along the Xingu River, one of the major tributaries of the Amazon River, are fighting to protect their land, which will be flooded if plans are carried out to build several enormous dams.

Africans also influenced Brazilian life. Three to 4 million Africans were brought to Brazil in the slave trade. When slavery was abolished in 1888, the freed slaves settled in agricultural areas, such as Bahia in the northeast, or in towns. The former slaves, who were mainly from West Africa, contributed to the cooking, art, music, language, religion, dress, folklore, and mining and farming techniques of Brazil.

Africa's influence on Brazil is shown in the rounded earth homes and brightly patterned decorations of the Kassena tribe, which reflect the Dahomey and other African cultures.

Immigrants from Portugal, Italy, Spain, Germany, and Poland and their descendants have given a European flavor to Brazil's population.

The third major ingredient of Brazilian culture came from the Portuguese, who accounted for the majority of emigrants from Europe for 300 years. The Portuguese are still immigrating to Brazil; 300,000 people who live in Brazil today were born in Portugal. The language, religion, customs, architecture, and family and political structures of Brazil derive mainly from Portugal.

Other immigrants have come from Italy, Germany, Spain, Poland, the Middle East, and Asia. Brazil has a large population of Japanese immigrants and their descendants; indeed, more people of Japanese descent live in Brazil than in any country outside Japan. Brazil has a long history of assimilation—that is, of incorporating various cultures into the whole. The result is a blend that is uniquely Brazilian. Although most Brazilians represent some degree of racial mixing, government statistics classify 53 percent of Brazilians as

Members of the African-Brazilian spiritist religions dress in white on New Year's Eve and head for the beaches to honor Iemanjá, goddess of the sea. Flowers, candles, and dancing commemorate the day.

white, 34 percent as mixed, 11 percent as African Brazilian, and the remaining 2 percent as Indians, Asians, and others.

Brazilians are aware of color differences, but economic class—that is, wealth or poverty—is more important than color in determining an individual's social status. Generally, however, the poorest people in Brazil tend to be the darker-skinned people with a large admixture of African or Native American ancestry. Many rural peasants, laborers, or city dwellers who cannot find jobs fall into this population category.

Religion

Religion is an integral part of Brazilian life, from personal saints and household shrines that form part of the domestic routine to ceremonies marking stages of life such as baptisms, marriages, and funerals. The country has a great many churches and chapels, and the frequent religious festivals function partly as entertainment for participants and spectators. Ninety percent of the people are Roman Catholic. This gives Brazil the largest Catholic population in the world. The Catholic church in Brazil is noted for its commitment to the poor. In addition to providing aid directly to the poor, the church has called on the government to bring about reforms in welfare, housing, education, and land distribution.

About six percent of Brazilians are Protestants from various churches: Lutheran, Anglican, Evangelical, Methodist, Baptist, Pentecostal, and Assembly of God. While most of the Protestant congregations are located in the cities, a few Protestant churches have set up missions to work with the rural people of the Northeast and other regions.

Liberation Theology is an important recent trend in both Catholic and Protestant churches throughout Latin America, including Brazil. In this movement to obtain justice for the poor and oppressed, members of the clergy and their followers become social activists—that is, they are actively involved in social and political causes. Religious social activists in Brazil have been subjected to prolonged imprisonment and other forms of repression for challenging the government. However, they have succeeded in drawing the attention of church members, environmentalists, and human rights organizations around the world to some of Brazil's problems.

In addition to Roman Catholic and Protestant churches, Brazil has Jews, Orthodox Christians, and Buddhists. There are also a number of spiritualists, whose religion is based on ideas about the spiritual world or the occult that were popular in Europe in the 19th century. Brazil is a tolerant land, hospitable to all forms of religions and religious cults.

One very widespread and uniquely Brazilian form of Spiritualism combines African deities, Catholic saints, and Indian practices. It is called Candomblé, Umbanda, Macumba, Quimbanda, or, more formally, African-Brazilian spiritism. About one-third of the people in Brazil, including many Roman Catholics, participate in these rituals or share these beliefs to some extent. The rites include dancing, singing, trances, and possession by spirits of the dead. Animal sacrifices are sometimes performed. Candomblé temples are particularly numerous in the state of Bahia, where the belief is strong.

Language

Brazilians are united by their language. Virtually everyone speaks Portuguese; Brazil is the largest Portuguese-speaking country in the world. But Brazilian Portuguese has approximately 10,000 more words than the language spoken in Portugal. Most of them were adopted from Indian and African languages. German, Italian, and Japanese are spoken by immigrant groups, while French and English are part of the studies of the well educated.

Quality of Life

The quality of life in Brazil depends on income. Half of the people in Brazil are considered to be poor by the economic standards of their own government. Generally, everyone in a poor family, including children, works at odd jobs or begs in order to contribute to the family income. About 35 million people live in favelas, the urban slums. Rio alone has 300 favelas. In 1984, 70 percent of Brazilians were malnourished. Because hunger is widespread, crowds of people loot supermarkets to get food; they have the sympathy of many political leaders.

The country's growing middle class is composed of millions of city dwellers who work for the government or for large businesses. They rent or buy modest apartments or houses with electricity, indoor bathrooms, and other conveniences. Their children attend school, whereas a great many poor children do not.

Wealth and political power are concentrated in a small fraction of the population. The richest one percent of the population, in fact,

(continued on page 65)

SCENES OF
BRAZIL

Overleaf: Children under 15 make up approximately 40 percent of Brazil's population.

Water drops into a chasm called the Devil's Throat at the Iguaçú Falls. Both Argentina and Brazil maintain national parks here.

Tropical trees, birds, fish, and aquatic animals flourish in the Mato Grosso wetlands, called the Pantanal. During the rainy season, the water level rises six feet (two meters) or more.

Wind erosion created these jagged rock formations in Paraná State.

Wooden stilts support houses along the Amazon, protecting them from seasonal flood-water. In the Amazon Basin, boats provide the most practical form of transportation.

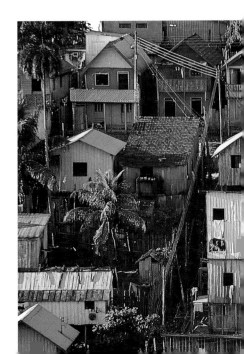

Twin skycrapers containing law offices dominate Brasília's congressional complex. To the right, *the domed section of the building houses Brazil's senate;* to the left, *the Chamber of Deputies meets beneath the inverted dome.*

Approximately 500,000 people live in close communities packed along the Rio Negro at Manaus, in the center of the Amazon Basin. Manaus is Brazil's largest inland city, exporting Brazil nuts, rubber, and hardwoods.

Volta Redonda, in Rio de Janeiro State, is Latin America's largest manufacturing city.

Petrópolis, a city just north of Rio de Janeiro, was a retreat for the emperor in the 19th century and remains an attractive, pastoral area. This is the cathedral of Petrópolis.

Tourists and native Brazilians alike enjoy the Portodo Barra beach in Salvador. Tourism has become a key factor in Brazil's economy.

The surprising yellow of the Federal Office Building is part of Brasília's innovative overall design.

Until recently, Brazil's Indian populations have been unaffected by industrialized civilization. Now, however, some are threatened. These Kaiapo Indians from the rain forest dress for their demonstration against the planned building of hydroelectric dams in the Amazon.

(continued from page 56)
receives about half of the country's income. Prosperous Brazilians live in expensive apartments or houses, often protected by armed guards. They are the top industrialists, politicians, military and government leaders, large landowners, and important religious and labor figures.

How People Earn Their Living

The working population consists of 61 million people, about 45 percent of the population. However, 62 percent of the population is within the working age of 15 to 64 years old. This means that 17 percent of the population is unemployed. Many working people are actually underemployed, taking part-time or odd jobs as they can. Brazil is considered to have a surplus of workers.

Since the 1950s, people have migrated in search of jobs. While most have moved to the cities, large numbers have also gone to new agricultural areas in the north, south, and west central regions. During the 1970s, more than 24 million people moved away from the towns where they were born.

In the rural areas, large plantations or ranches are owned by the rich; however, the farm workers are poor. One-third of the employed work in agricultural jobs. Most farmers cultivate such crops as coffee, cocoa, soybeans, and sugarcane for the plantation owners, but some have their own small farms and grow food for their families and for sale in local markets. Other agricultural jobs involve working on cattle ranches, lumbering, and rubber tapping. The coast and the large rivers have small fishing industries.

About one percent of the workers are involved in mining for iron, manganese (used in making metal alloys), bauxite (aluminum), gold, and other ores. Manufacturing industries employ 16 percent of the workers in the production of steel, machinery, vehicles, weapons, processed food, chemicals, plastics, clothing, shoes, and furniture. Another 28 percent of the working population provides community, social, and personal services. Government workers, teachers, doctors, lawyers, domestic servants, postal workers, and scores of other occupations are included in this category. About four percent of the workers are employed in the transportation and communications industries, and five percent work in finance, insurance, and real estate. Business and trade occupy 10 percent of those employed. The remaining workers are involved in construction and other jobs.

Cuisine and Clothing

Cooking differs widely from region to region, depending on each area's history and culture. The cuisine of Bahia, which has a strong African flavor, is famous for combining fish, shrimp, or chicken with vegetables in a spicy, peppery sauce; palm oil also figures in the dishes of this area, as it does in many West African foods. Brazil's national dish, popular throughout the country, is *feijoada*, which is a stew of black beans, sausage, beef, and pork, served with rice, kale, orange slices, and sautéed manioc flour. It is prepared in thousands of local versions.

A typical breakfast consists of *café com leite* (coffee with milk), bread and jam, and fresh fruit. Lunch is the largest meal, often consisting of rice, beans, and meat, chicken, or seafood. A light meal is eaten in the evening. Brazilians enjoy morning and afternoon snacks, stopping at cafés, luncheonettes, or food stands for cookies, bread, or highly salted fried dough with meat or sweet fillings. *Cafezinho*, strong sweet coffee, is a favorite beverage for adults. Sweet desserts are popular.

A variety of liquids are consumed: soft drinks, bottled water, rum, beer, and local wines. A very popular carbonated soft drink is *guarana*, made from a berry. A bitter herb called *maté* is made into *chimarrão*, a tea drunk by the gauchos from a hollow gourd through a metal straw.

Clothing in Brazil is similar to that seen in the warmer parts of the United States; people dress for comfort and the climate. Bikinis

Thirty-five million people, more than 20 percent of the population, live in favelas like this one. There are more than 300 favelas in Rio de Janeiro alone.

are popular on the beaches. Two styles of the brief bathing suits are called *tanga* (string) and *fio dental* (dental floss). There are also traditional regional outfits. In Bahia, African-Brazilian women wear long, colorful skirts with bright blouses and many bracelets. Candomblé priestesses wear white clothes and turbans or other festive headdresses. Gauchos wear baggy trousers, high leather boots, bandannas around their necks, wide hats, and large bands of leather around their waists for protection from the cattle. Costumes worn for the annual Carnaval festival are elaborate, beautiful, and expensive, featuring mirrors, feathers, metallic cloth and silk, and sometimes even gems and coins.

Customs

Brazilians hug and kiss one another and shake hands often. The *abraço*, or embrace, is a common greeting among friends and relatives. Brazilians regard family life as extremely important, and most people include even somewhat distant relatives as kin. Events such as baptisms, weddings, funerals, birthdays, and other milestones are honored by these relatives, who may number in the hundreds. Mutual help and support among members of these large families has been customary in Brazil, but current trends in migration have caused many family members to live apart from each other. This may be weakening the traditional family structure.

In traditional Brazilian culture, the ideal family consists of a man who is master of the house and protects and provides for his family; a woman who is a respectful wife and a devoted mother; and obedient children. In reality, however, urban middle-class and lower-class families often differ from this model. And while men have authority over women in the family, the trend today is toward more equality between the sexes. Women gained the right to vote in 1932, and the 1988 constitution granted them additional rights, including four-month maternity leave from their jobs. Divorce has been legal since 1977. The teaching profession was the first to be available to women. Today, many women are found in all the

In a rural community, near the coastal city of Recife, a potter earns his livelihood using handmade tools and traditional methods.

professions, in the arts, and in government. In 1988, a woman was elected mayor of São Paulo. There are three kinds of marriages in Brazil: civil, religious, and common law. Civil marriage is the only one recognized by law. Women often marry at 17 or 18 years of age. Typically, young couples set up housekeeping with some financial help from their parents. The average family today has two or three children; families were much larger in the past. Multigenerational households are common, especially in the south, with grand-parents, parents, and children—maybe even grandchildren—all living under one roof. Parents hoping to help their children get off to a good start in life give them an education, some land, or money. Later in life, the children will be responsible for helping their parents in their old age. *Compadrio*, or godparenthood, is taken very seriously. Its obligations involve the child, the parents, and the godparents and is considered to be lifelong.

Holidays

The Brazilian calendar is filled with holidays, many of them religious in origin. The most famous and spectacular is Carnaval, which is celebrated for four days and five nights before Lent. In preparation for Carnaval, the samba schools (or clubs) from the favelas choose themes, write samba music and lyrics, create elab-orate costumes and floats, and practice for the big event. The best clubs are chosen to compete in the parade. While Carnaval is celebrated in many cities in Brazil, Rio's is the best known. Tourists come from all over the world to join the party. In 1984, Rio built the huge Sambodromo to accommodate people watching the parade. Lavish fancy dress balls and parties at homes are also customary.

Tiradentes's Day, April 21, honors the father of Brazilian inde-pendence, Joaquim José da Silva Xavier. Christmas Day, December 25, is celebrated traditionally in small towns with plays, dancing, and singing. In the large cities, it is similar to European and American Christmas festivities, with church services, decorations,

Copacabana Beach in Rio de Janeiro features black-and-white tile sidewalks in wave patterns modeled on mosaics found in Lisbon, the capital of Portugal.

and exchanges of gifts. Papai Noel (Father Christmas) visits in São Paulo and Rio in his traditional beard, red suit, and hat, although the season is summer and the weather hot.

On New Year's Eve, followers of African-Brazilian spiritist religions honor Iemanjá, goddess of the sea. Dressed in white, celebrants travel to the beaches with flowers, candles, and gifts. They sing and dance around open fires on the beaches. In some places, fireworks light the skies. At midnight, the offerings are cast into the waves. If Iemanjá accepts the gifts, it is a sign that the coming year will be a good one. It is a bad omen, however, if the gifts are returned to the shore.

Other holidays are New Year's Day, January 1; Good Friday; Easter Sunday; Labor Day, May 1; Independence Day, September 7; the day of Our Lady of Aparecida, Patroness of Brazil, October 12;

All Souls Day, November 2; and Proclamation of the Republic Day, November 15. Several saints' days are celebrated during June; together they are called the June Festivals. In addition, there are many local holidays.

Sports and Pastimes

Soccer is a national pastime, and boys start to play when they are very young. Rio's huge Maracanã soccer stadium, the largest in the world, seats 200,000. World Cup games are played every four years. Pelé, a Brazilian soccer star who has retired from the game, is considered the best soccer player in history.

Capoeira is a Brazilian sport with a West African background that combines dancing and foot fighting. Participants must be fast, agile, and accurate in their steps. Music provides a rhythmic background for the performers.

Beaches are an important part of life. Many activities take place there—few people swim, but many splash in the waves or bathe in the sun. Volleyball games spring up, and active sports such as waterskiing, surfing, windsurfing, and hang gliding are popular. Boating and fishing are part of the leisurely life of some coastal dwellers.

Brazilians also enjoy watching sports events, especially basketball, volleyball, boxing, tennis, horse races, and automobile races. The Grand Prix auto races are an exciting annual event.

Music and dance are key ingredients in Brazilian life and expression. Many people are skilled dancers, and dance clubs are numerous and well attended. Samba, the national music, has its roots in African music and has evolved over the centuries, incorporating music from other ethnic groups. It is a very rich tradition, close to the heart. Its lyrics can carry messages of poetry, protest, or parody. This is the music of Carnaval, exploding with energy. The samba, the bossa nova, and other forms of Brazilian popular music and dance are recognized and enjoyed around the world.

Luis Ignacio da Silva (center, speaking) founded the Workers party and ran for governor of the state of São Paulo in 1982. A union organizer in a country where strikes were then illegal, he tested the limits of Brazil's democracy and was compared to Lech Walesa of Poland.

5

Government and Social Services

The Federative Republic of Brazil (República Federativa do Brasil) is a constitutional republic—that is, a state based on a constitution with power residing in the citizens who vote. It has a strong central, or federal, government.

The country is divided into 23 states, 3 territories, and a federal district that includes the capital, Brasília. The states are further divided into municipalities and districts. State governments are similar to the federal government; each has a constitution, a head of state (governor), state assemblies, and state court systems. Municipalities are similar to counties in the United States and are headed by mayors. Rural districts can be upgraded to municipalities when their populations are sufficiently large.

Branches of Government

The function of the executive branch of government—the president and his cabinet of advisers and administrators—is to oversee the economy, international relations, and national defense. The president appoints ministers to head 26 departments that administer such areas as agriculture, the army, education, health, and labor. These ministers form the cabinet.

The legislative branch of government, or congress, makes the laws, approves international treaties, decides some administrative matters, and can authorize the president to declare war. The congress has two houses: the Senate and the Chamber of Deputies. There are 72 members of the Senate: 3 from each state and 1 from each territory. The membership of the Chamber of Deputies is based on the population of the various states and districts. At the time of the 1989 elections, it totaled 479. Deputies are elected for four-year terms, senators for eight-year terms.

The judiciary branch of government administers justice through the court system. The 11 justices of the Federal Supreme Court are appointed for life by the president; his appointments must be approved by the Senate. There are lower federal courts in the states, territories, and federal district. Throughout the country is a system of state, local, and military courts. In the past, judicial decisions could be overruled by the president; the courts are more independent under the new constitution.

Constitution

A new constitution went into effect in September 1988. It establishes that the government will be headed by a president, elected for a term of five years. The constitution creates a division of power between the government and the military—formerly, the military controlled the government. The constitution also gives more power and a larger share of the federal tax income to the states than was the case under the former constitution. The president cannot issue laws or make formal proclamations (statements of major government policy, such as declaring war or imposing martial law) without the approval of the congress.

Some laws concerning labor were changed when the new constitution was written. The work week was reduced from 48 to 44 hours, and strikes are now legal. Parents have the right to maternity and paternity leaves.

Political Parties

Brazil's political parties embrace various philosophies. The Brazilian Democratic Movement party (PMDB) wants government by the people, rather than the military; the Social Democratic party (PDS) has supported the military in the past; and the Liberal Front party (PFL) has broken away from the PDS over the support of some candidates. A new party, the Brazilian Social Democrats party (PSDB), was formed by politicians from São Paulo who broke away from PMDB. Other parties include the Democratic Transition Bloc, which is the party of José Sarney and some left-wing (liberal or radical socialist and communist) groups. In addition, there are a few groups organized around special interests, particular issues, or

Brazil has the largest military force in Latin America, spending about U.S. $1 billion annually on defense.

well-liked figures. In general, there seems to be a shift to the political left—that is, toward socialistic or communistic political theories—and a feeling that the common people need a government that will act in their interest.

Military and Police Forces

Men between the ages of 18 and 45 are required to serve in the armed forces for 1 year. Although women and the clergy are not required to become soldiers, all Brazilians are responsible for supporting national security in an emergency. There are three branches of the service: army, navy, and air force. The country's total military personnel is 283,400—the largest armed forces in Latin America. They are well supplied with military equipment and are kept in a state of combat readiness, even though they have not been under arms since World War II. Competition for top officer positions is rigorous and keen. Defense spending is in the neighborhood of U.S. $1 billion a year.

The first national elections in 21 years were held in 1985, ending military control of the government and paving the streets of São Paulo with campaign materials.

Police agencies operate at the federal and state levels, with a total of 240,000 police (1 for every 465 people). The Department of Federal Police is very powerful. It is responsible for controlling air, sea, and border traffic; for stopping narcotics trade; and for maintaining national security. The department also stores and provides intelligence information, assists the state police, and cooperates with the International Criminal Police Organization (Interpol). Two other police agencies in the Ministry of Transportation and Public Works are responsible for patrolling railways and highways.

There are three types of state police—military, civil, and traffic—and all have close ties to the federal forces. In addition to the usual police equipment, the military police are heavily armed and have machine guns and tanks. They can function as additional armed forces, if needed, in an emergency. Fire fighting is part of their duties.

The civil police handle criminal cases and security. There are no city, or municipal, police departments; each state is organized into precincts rather than cities. Because of the extreme poverty, street crime is becoming more frequent. In Rio alone there were 537 murders in the month of April 1989, many of them connected with the drug trade. In general, however, Brazilian crime statistics are not reliable because many crimes go unreported.

Voting and Human Rights

Brazilians are obliged to vote. Men and working women who are 16 to 65 years old must cast their vote. People over 65, women who do not work, and military officers may choose to vote or not. Enlisted members of the armed forces cannot vote or run for office. The country has 30 million registered voters.

Brazil is moving toward more rights and freedoms for individuals. For many years, particularly in the period from 1964 to 1982, the military government was noted for the repression of civil rights and for its refusal to tolerate any opposition to its policies.

Imprisonment and brutal treatment, including torture, were used to quell dissent. Death squads, largely made up of policemen on their own time, murdered people whom they considered to be criminals, terrorists, or revolutionaries until the government stopped them. Although there have been improvements in human rights, Brazil has not yet signed the Inter-American Convention on Human Rights. However, human rights organizations have freely visited Brazil, although attempts to interfere with the affairs of the government are not welcome.

Education

Education in Brazil is compulsory, or required by law, for children 7 to 14 years old. Thorough enforcement of this law is impossible, however, and many poor children do not attend school. The school year runs from March to December; instruction is in Portuguese. In some schools, youngsters can choose to attend school in the morning or in the afternoon; after fifth grade, evening classes are available.

The first level of required schooling is primary school, which is divided into eight grades. For the first four years, children study reading and arithmetic in a combined program. In the fifth through eighth years, the course of study includes Portuguese, science, mathematics, social studies, and vocational subjects. Generally, only some city schools offer a full range of subjects, whereas schools in poor neighborhoods or in rural areas offer fewer choices.

Middle school lasts three or four years. There are two tracks: academic and vocational. The academic course prepares students for higher education, while the vocational teaches employment skills needed in the labor market. About 20 percent of adolescents 15 to 19 years old attend middle school. Students must complete 1,000 hours of instruction, and can do so at their own pace, rather than in a set number of years. Academic subjects include language, Brazilian literature, social studies, mathematics, and science. Voca-

Brazil's powerful police forces have been guilty of human rights abuses. These men were arrested and roped for not carrying ID cards; they were later released, and the police chief was fired. Brazil's new constitution, which went into effect in 1988, was designed to give citizens protection from such mistreatment.

tional areas are industry, agriculture, primary education, service occupations, and commerce, which is the most popular course of study.

Higher education is offered at 65 colleges and universities. Entrance examinations are very difficult, and students enroll in special private schools to study for them. Class sizes average 25 pupils in primary school, 14 in middle school, and 12 in college. Although teachers have considerable social status, their salaries are low.

The Brazilian government estimates that 75 percent of adults can read and write—a figure of 40 percent, however, may be closer to reality. Some people were never fully able to read, and others have lost the ability through lack of practice. But in recent years a

Brazil's few colleges have small enrollments, so competition for college admission is fierce. The results of the national exams are published in the newspapers. This happy high school senior made it through the first round.

large-scale adult education program, which offers five monthlong evening courses, has taught several million people to read. The program is funded by the lottery and by contributions from businesses. Another successful adult education program has been vocational training for young adults and the unemployed.

The country's economic problems have affected the educational system. Budgets have been cut, with a result that the quality of education has declined. In general, the schools are not adequate for the needs of a modern industrial country.

Health Care

Health services and life expectancy vary greatly depending on economic status and the region of the country. Cities have more services than the interior or rural regions. About 40 percent of Brazilians do not have access to health services, although a new health and welfare program called Prevsaude was started in 1981 to improve health care. The average life expectancy for women is 66 years; for men it is 61 years. The infant mortality rate is 70 per 1,000 live births—this means that 70 of every 1,000 babies die during their first year. However, this rate varies with economic class and is much higher for Brazil's slum population than for the upper class. In general, poor sanitation, unreliable water supplies, malnutrition, and environmental conditions such as pollution contribute to the health problems of the population.

Tropical countries have many parasitic diseases. In Brazil, such diseases cause 16 percent of the deaths. Parasites live inside a host animal or person, causing a variety of illnesses. A parasite can be a single-celled creature or any one of many types of worms. It is estimated that half the population of Brazil may be infested with one or more parasites, and nearly everyone in the northeast region is infested. The most common parasitic diseases are malaria, Chagas' disease, and schistosomiasis.

One-quarter of all deaths in Brazil are caused by respiratory diseases such as pneumonia, tuberculosis, and influenza. Another 25 percent are caused by diseases that affect the heart and blood vessels. Other major causes of death are malnutrition (which affects one-third of the population), cancer, and communicable diseases such as dysentery, tuberculosis, measles, whooping cough, and syphilis. Meningitis sometimes occurs in epidemic proportions. Leprosy, typhoid fever, tetanus, and AIDS also present serious health problems. In 1988, 4,439 cases of AIDS were reported, and health experts expect this fatal disease to spread rapidly in Brazil as it has done in other countries.

Brazil has about 110,000 doctors, 60,000 dentists, and 23,000 nurses. Half the physicians practice in Rio and São Paulo; many of the remaining doctors are found in other cities, and relatively few are found in the country. Paramedics, who have some medical training, serve as health care workers in rural areas.

Brazil is rich in natural resources and has been one of the world's leaders in gold and diamond mining. Today, Brazil has the world's largest emerald reserve. Economic conditions force thousands of men, women, and children to the emerald fields each year; this woman hopes that one of the rocks she has sifted will be worth a fortune.

6

Economy, Transportation, and Communication

Brazil currently suffers from economic problems that affect the life of nearly all Brazilian people and drive political events. The major factors in the troubled economy are the large foreign debt, the high rate of inflation, and the unequal distribution of wealth.

But Brazil has many natural resources. There are large forest reserves and vast river systems used for transportation and as a source of electrical energy. The country's iron-ore deposits are the second largest in the world. Its bauxite, manganese, and gold deposits are among the world's largest. Other mineral riches include copper, lead, tungsten, tin, silver, and diamonds. Platinum has recently been discovered. However, Brazil is deficient in coal, oil, and natural gas.

If the history of Brazil's economy were drawn on a chart, it would look like a roller-coaster ride. It has been a series of boom-and-bust cycles. The boom occurs when Brazil leads the world in the production of a single product and sells this product to other nations at good prices. The bust follows when the world market for that product collapses due to oversupply or to depression and prices fall. Brazil's "boom" products have included sugar, gold, diamonds, cotton, cocoa, rubber, and—most recently—coffee. Today, the price of coffee on the world market continues to affect the well-being of the economy. When coffee sells for high prices, Brazil's earnings increase; when the price of coffee slumps, however, Brazil's earnings drop and the supply of money within the country is reduced.

Manufacturing

Brazil has become increasingly industrial and is ranked as the eighth-largest industrial nation in the world. The major manufacturing locality is in the south, in the area of São Paulo, Rio de Janeiro, and Belo Horizonte. Brazil is the leading car manufacturer in Latin America; Volkswagen of Brazil is responsible for half the cars that emerge from its factories. Shipbuilding, airplane construction, and the arms and military-equipment industries are growing. Brazil produces electrical equipment such as television sets, radios, refrigerators, air conditioners, and computers. It refines oil to produce petroleum products such as gasoline, kerosene, and synthetic rubber. The production of alcohol, which is mixed with gasoline to make a fuel called gasohol, is increasing.

The government of Brazil has a large role in manufacturing. Many companies are owned, operated, or controlled by the government. The aircraft and soda-ash industries are completely state run. The computer and robotics industry is rapidly growing and is protected by federal agencies.

Mining

Brazil leads the world in iron ore exports. Other important mining products are bauxite, coal, manganese, tin, lead, dolomite, sea salt, gold, and silver. Diamonds and gemstones are mined, as are high-quality quartz crystals.

An oil field off the shore of Rio de Janeiro produces some of the oil that Brazil needs. Another strike has been made at Urucu, 1,450 miles (2,320 kilometers) up the Amazon River, but it has not yet been put into production. In order to develop the Urucu oil field, which will probably yield only .3 percent of Brazil's petroleum needs, teams of workers must be flown into the jungle by helicopter to clear the trees. Drilling equipment is then flown in on enormous helicopters and assembled for use. A large natural-gas field has been found close to Urucu, but it has not been developed because it is located too far from potential users.

Agriculture

Most agricultural land is in the form of large parcels owned by a few people or corporations, with the top 2 percent of the large landowners owning 60 percent of the farmland. This state of affairs dates from early in the history of Brazil, when Portugal awarded large land grants as captaincies. About 70 percent of the rural families are landless.

The Amazon region is viewed as a target for the establishment of large farms, ranches, and lumbering operations even though the soil will not support these uses for more than a few years. In addition, the very existence of the world's largest tropical rain forest is threatened. Once destroyed for cultivation, the jungle environment will probably never return. Although other countries have offered their help in trying to protect this unique resource, Brazil resents foreign intervention. It appears increasingly likely that the Amazon rain forest will fall to fuel Brazil's economic growth.

Many crops grow well in Brazil's climate. The major crops are coffee, cotton, corn, beans, rice, cassava, wheat, potatoes, soybeans, sugarcane, cocoa, oranges, tobacco, bananas, peanuts, and rubber. Other important crops are Brazil nuts, sisal, castor beans, pineapples, pepper, and maté tea. Even though large crops of wheat, rice, and corn are grown, Brazil does not produce enough of these items—which are basic to the diet of Brazilians—to meet its needs. Substantial quantities of them must be imported.

Brazil has 93 million cattle (one-fourth of all the world's cattle), 36 million pigs, 17.5 million sheep, 8 million goats, and 400 million chickens. Although Brazil is a major beef producer, much of the beef is consumed within the country, and little is exported. In addition, horses, mules, asses, and buffalo are raised. Animal products such as eggs, milk, and wool account for important segments of the nation's overall income from livestock production.

Forests cover about half of the land area of Brazil and yield many products. Hardwood and softwood lumber are used locally as well as exported. Some of the trees come from the Amazon, although much of the forest is still inaccessible—a situation that will change when a planned Trans-Amazon Highway is finished. Other trees

One-fourth of the world's cattle are found on Brazilian ranches. Most of the beef produced is consumed in Brazil, and the leather is used in the country's important footwear industry.

are cultivated. Brazil's forests respond well to extractive procedures, in which products are harvested without damage to the plants. Rubber, waxes and oils, Brazil nuts, maté, and fibers form the bulk of these extracted products. Vanilla, cloves, cinnamon, and cocoa have also been collected.

Although there are extensive fishing grounds off the coast of Brazil and in the rivers, the fishing industry is underdeveloped. Lobsters are the only seafood currently exported.

Tourism and Trade

Two million visitors a year from around the world enjoy the beautiful sights of Brazil and contribute to its economy. In particular, the spectacular Carnaval in Rio attracts people who join in the celebration of a uniquely Brazilian event.

Brazil engages in trade with countries around the world. It has been strengthening the economic relationships among neighboring countries and would like to establish a Latin American common market—a trade agreement similar to the European Community (EC). The United States is Brazil's major trading partner. Other partners include Argentina, France, Great Britain, Italy, Japan, the Netherlands, Saudi Arabia, and West Germany. The Brazilian arms industry is growing at a fast pace and accounts for a growing percentage of the country's export production. Brazil supplies Libya, Saudi Arabia, and other nations with munitions.

Brazil consumes about 500,000 barrels of oil a day. Half of this oil is imported. Other necessary imports include chemicals, fertilizers, wheat, and machinery.

Coffee is the major food export. Other agricultural products that are exported are soybeans, oranges, orange juice, sugar, cocoa, tobacco, poultry, and livestock. Iron ore, iron and steel, arms, automobiles, trucks, hats, and shoes are mined or manufactured for foreign markets.

Foreign Debt

Brazil has a large foreign debt of about $115 billion. The debt exists because the government has borrowed heavily from other nations and from international banks in order to build roads and bridges and to encourage industrial growth. The country has struggled to pay the interest on this debt, which amounts to U.S. $14 billion a year, and doing so has hurt the country financially. Along with other Latin American countries that are in the same situation, Brazil is looking for solutions and help from other nations, including the United States. Possible solutions are to exchange the debt for investments in Brazilian companies; to spend only what is taken in taxes, and not go further into debt; or to stop paying interest for a time. Brazil needs the money for economic growth, which has dropped to less than one percent a year. One effect of Brazil's financial woes is the bankruptcy of the city of Rio de Janeiro in 1989.

Units of Currency

Currency has been devalued over the years because of inflation. The cruzado, introduced in February 1986, replaced the cruzeiro, with 1 cruzado being worth 1,000 cruzeiros. A "new cruzado" was introduced in 1988. This brought an additional devaluation, or decrease in the buying power of currency.

The average household income was equal to U.S. $254 in 1964, to U.S. $700 in 1970, and to U.S. $2,370 in 1989. These figures do not give a true picture, however, because there is a vast disparity between the rich and the poor. Very few households earn the "average" income; a handful earn much more, and many earn much less. Half of Brazil's people live on family incomes of U.S. $50 or less a month.

Current Economic Problems

In addition to the large foreign debt, Brazil's inflation (a situation in which prices rise and the value of money decreases) has affected the economy for many years. For a long time, the inflation rate was

More than 16 million children live on the streets and must sell whatever they can find or steal to survive.

close to 100 percent a year. In 1988 it reached 934 percent, and President Sarney warned of the possibility of hyperinflation—that is, of an inflation rate that might reach 1,500 percent. A wage and price freeze and further devaluation of the cruzado were announced. The government hoped thus to reduce inflation. However, like previous attempts at wage and price freezes, these measures did not have the needed effect. The inflation rate continues to rise as Brazil enters the 1990s.

Transportation

Brazilian highways handle 70 percent of the freight and 90 percent of the passenger traffic in the country. There are 869,052 miles (1,399,440 kilometers) of roads; 52,142 miles (83,965 kilometers) are paved, and the rest are dirt or gravel. The 2 major highway-construction projects are the 3,105-mile (5,000-kilometer) Trans-Amazon Highway, which will run from the Atlantic coast to the border of Peru, and the Northern Perimeter Road, which will run north of the Amazon for 2,600 miles (4,183 kilometers). Brazilians have 9,921,887 private cars and 1,144,614 commercial vehicles.

Inland waterways are the main source of transportation in the Amazon Basin, where nearly every family has a boat.

Brazil does not have a national system of railroads. The federal government, state governments, and private businesses own various lines. In 1973 the first transcontinental railroad was built. It runs from Santos, the port of São Paulo, across the Andes Mountains to Chile, linking the Atlantic and Pacific oceans. There are plans to construct more lines and to improve the railway systems, if funds can be found to do so.

Air travel is necessary to reach many parts of the country. Brazil has 4,000 airfields; 220 are paved, and 126 offer regularly scheduled flights. The airports at Rio de Janeiro, São Paulo, and seven other cities handle international flights. Brazilian airlines have a reputation for safety and good service. More than 2,000 passengers a day use the popular "air bridge," a commuter flight between Rio and São Paulo. During rush hours, a flight leaves every half hour.

Water transportation and shipping are very important. Brazil has the world's largest inland waterway system, some 31,000 miles (50,000 kilometers) long. Although more than half the large-scale commercial shipping activity takes place in the southern rivers, near the major cities, inland waterways are the main form of transportation in the Amazon Basin, where nearly every family owns a small boat, a canoe, or a dugout made of a hollowed-out log. The Amazon and its tributaries are the principal highways for these "pickup trucks of the Amazon," as they have been called, and business and social life depends upon water transport.

Brazil has 700 river ports, 90 of which are used for commercial shipping. The country also has 8 major and 23 minor seaports. Rio is the center of shipping, handling 40 percent of the goods transported by water. Santos handles another 30 percent.

Media and Communications

The National Telecommunications Department of the federal government licenses and regulates radio and television broadcasting. Most of the 2,073 radio stations are privately owned businesses, but a few are operated by the government or the Catholic church. There are 67 million radios in Brazil, and 36 million television sets.

Between 50 and 70 movies are produced each year in Brazil. By law, every movie theater must show one Brazilian film for every eight foreign films. Moviegoing is very popular—215 million tickets are sold each year.

There are 328 newspapers in Brazil, with a total circulation of 5,094,000. Most are written in Portuguese, although two daily papers are in English. Foreign ownership of newspapers is prohibited by law. No one newspaper is distributed nationally. The papers with the largest circulations are published in Rio de Janeiro and in São Paulo; that with the lowest circulation, the *Correio Brasiliense*, comes from Brasília. The *Diario de Pernambuco*, founded in 1825, claims to be the oldest newspaper in Latin America. The popular illustrated magazine *O Cruzeiro*, which is published in Rio, is circulated throughout Latin America in a special Spanish-language edition. Brazil also has more than 100 publishing companies that produce a total of about 13,000 new books each year.

Two Warriors, *by Brazil's best-known sculptor, Bruno Georgi, greets visitors to Brasília, the capital city.*

7

Arts and Culture

Many of the themes and images used by creative artists and musicians come from Brazilian life, people, and tradition. Brazil stirs the imagination and invites consideration of its richness and paradoxes. While the main influences have been African, Indian, and Portuguese, other ethnic groups have contributed sounds and images as well.

Literature

One of Brazil's greatest writers and a master of the Portuguese language, Joaquim Maria Machado de Assis (1839–1908), depicted everyday Brazilian life in his novels. *The Posthumous Memoirs of Braz Cubas*, *Epitaph for a Small Winner*, and *Don Casmurro* are some of his best-known works. He also wrote plays and lyric poetry. Despite poverty, epilepsy, and little formal education, Machado de Assis became a world-renowned literary figure.

Around the world, the single best known book by a Brazilian author is probably *Os Sertões* (called *Rebellion in the Backlands* in English), by Euclides da Cunha (1866–1909). It not only recounts the army's quelling of an uprising but is also a study of the relationship of society with "the interior," the vast frontier area that has an almost mystical meaning to Brazilians.

João Guimãraes Rosa (1908–67) continued the analysis of the meaning of the interior begun by da Cunha. In *The Devil to Pay in the Backlands*, the country's interior is compared to a human mind and soul. The stories in his collection *Sagarana* are considered masterpieces. A popular contemporary author is Jorge Amado (b. 1912), who writes earthy, engaging novels that tell stories about the common people of Bahia, the predominantly African-Brazilian state of the northeast. Amado's characters are clever, amusing, and full of life. His works have been translated into 31 languages, and several of his novels have been made into movies. Amado's novels include *The Violent Land*, *Gabriela, Clove and Cinnamon*, and *Dona Flor and Her Two Husbands*.

Other novelists are Rachel de Queirós (b. 1910), who at the age of 19 wrote *The Year Fifteen* about living through a drought; Graciliamo Ramos (1892–1953); José Lins do Rêgo (1901–57); and Clarice Lispector (b. 1922). Contemporary Brazilian writers include João Ubaldo Ribeiro, author of *An Invisible Memory*; Murilo Rubião, author of *The Ex-Magician and Other Stories*; and Marcio Souza, author of *Emperor of the Amazon*.

The poet Casimiro de Abreu (1837–60) lived for a while in Portugal but longed for Brazil. Most Brazilians can recite his poem "Meus Oito Anos" ("When I Was Eight Years Old"). Manuel Bandeira (1886–1968) is the most respected "great old man" of Brazilian poetry; his best-known work is a poem about his boyhood in Recife. Cecília Meireles (1901–65) was another major poet. Other important 20th-century poets are João Cabral de Melo Neto, Carlos Drummond de Andrade, and Vinícius de Morais, who wrote the play upon which the film *Black Orpheus* was based.

Gilberto de Mello Freyre (b. 1900) has analyzed Brazilian society, defined its unique qualities, and made it comprehensible to Brazilians and the world. His books include *The Masters and the*

Jorge Amado (left) writes novels about the African-Brazilian culture of Bahia. His books are popular all over the world. Here he chats with Argentine writer Julio Cortazar at a book fair in West Germany.

Slaves, The Mansions and the Shanties, and *Mother and Son: A Brazilian Tale*. Paulo Freire (b. 1921), an educator and author, has promoted adult literacy. He wrote *Pedagogy of the Oppressed* and other books about education.

Although some excellent plays have been produced in Brazil, theatrical development was hampered by censorship between the 1950s and the 1980s. Ariano Suassuna (b. 1927) is considered one of Brazil's leading playwrights. He wrote *The Rogue's Trial*, a satirical look at some of Brazil's problems. Alfredo Dias Gomes (b. 1924) wrote the play *To Pay Vows*, which was made into a film. João Cabral de Melo Neto dramatized his poem "The Death and Life of Severino."

Artists

São Paulo encourages artistic development with its Biennale, which is world renowned and very competitive. It is a major art exhibit that occurs every two years. Four thousand works of art are shown in a hall a mile long.

One of Brazil's best-known artists of the 18th century was Antônio Francisco Lisboa (1739–1814), known as Aleijadinho (Little Cripple), who designed churches and sculpted beautiful statues of religious figures. He worked with his tools strapped to his hands, which were disabled (perhaps because of leprosy). Some contemporary artists are Manabu Mabe (b. 1924), a Japanese Brazilian who works in an abstract style, Lasar Segall (1891–1957), and Emiliano di Calvalcanti (b. 1897). Particularly well known are Tarsila do

Paintings are exhibited at an art fair in São Paulo. Brazil's rich mix of European, African, and native Indian cultures inspires equally diverse and imaginative works of art.

Amaral (b. 1890) and Cândido Portinari (1903–62), whose murals hang in the United Nations General Assembly in New York City and the Library of Congress in Washington, D.C. Bruno Georgi (b. 1905) is Brazil's top sculptor; his statue *Two Warriors* stands in Brasília.

Architecture

Brazil has a history of handsome, well-constructed buildings, from *fazendas* (estate houses) to highly decorated churches. In some towns, houses and churches are ornamented with ceramic tiles. In addition to preserving examples of traditional architecture, Brazil has encouraged modern architecture. An outstanding example is the Palace of Culture in Rio, designed by Le Corbusier and Lúcio Costa; it was built in 1945 on concrete pillars. The capital city of Brasília was planned by Lúcio Costa, with many of its buildings designed by the noted architect Oscar Niemeyer (b. 1907) in a very contemporary style. Modern sculptures, considered quite daring and advanced in the 1960s, complement the city's architecture. Roberto Burle Marx (b. 1909), an award-winning landscape architect, designed the gardens around the Museum of Modern Art in Rio.

Museums and Libraries

There are 409 museums in Brazil, mostly in the large cities. In Rio, the National Museum has a fine collection of Indian and scientific material. The National Museum of Fine Arts has a large collection of paintings and sculpture and also exhibits the works of current artists. The Museum of Modern Art was damaged in a fire in 1978; the building is being restored and the collection is being built up again with the help of gifts from other countries. The Historical Museum has artworks, furniture, maps, and other objects from Brazil's past. In São Paulo, the Museum of Art has European masterpieces as well as fine examples of Brazilian art. The Museum of Contemporary Art specializes in modern work.

The Goeldi Museum in Belém has many artifacts from Amazonian life and history, including a collection of Marajo Indian pottery. A zoo with anacondas and other animals and a garden exhibiting local plants are located on the museum grounds.

São Paulo has the country's largest municipal library system, with a million volumes. The National Library in Rio has 1.8 million volumes and many rare manuscripts.

Music

Brazil's history of music started with the Jesuits, who brought sacred music to the country and taught the Indians to perform it. Today, Brazil has many talented musicians, music schools, concerts, bars and restaurants with live music—and, of course, Carnaval. Many types of music are heard: classical, samba, bossa nova, rock, and contemporary instrumental music.

Popular music has been a vehicle to protest government actions; during the more repressive regimes, in fact, outspoken musicians have been jailed and their music banned. Many poets have written lyrics for music. Brazilian popular music has spread around the world and currently influences rock groups such as David Byrne's Talking Heads.

Two outstanding individuals in the musical field are Antonio Carlos Gomes (1836–96), who wrote operas in the 19th century (his *Il Guarany* was performed at the renowned La Scala opera house in Milan, Italy), and Heitor Villa-Lobos (1887–1959), the greatest figure in Brazilian music, who used traditional Brazilian themes and sounds. Many talented Brazilian composers, singers, conductors, ballerinas, guitarists, and pianists have performed on the continent and abroad.

Movies

There are thousands of movie theaters in Brazil. Cinema is a thriving industry and a popular art form. Some of the better-known films that have been produced in Brazil are *Gaijin*, *Pixote*, *Bye-Bye Brazil*, and *Kiss of the Spider Woman*. The makers of documentary films have tried to capture the beauty and the suffering of Brazilian life.

Two Brazilian actresses have become well known in North America. They are Carmen Miranda and Sonia Braga. Miranda (1909–55) sang and danced in Hollywood musicals. Her trademark was elaborate costumes topped with huge hats or headdresses, which sometimes were decorated with tropical fruit. She appeared in *Copacabana* (1947), *A Date with Judy* (1950), and *Nancy Goes to Rio* (1950). The Carmen Miranda Museum in Rio has a collection of her gowns and other items. Braga has acted in a number of Brazilian films and has become an international star who is admired for both beauty and acting ability. *Dona Flor and Her Two Husbands*, *Kiss of the Spider Woman*, *The Milagro Beanfield War*, and *Moon Over Parador* are among her films.

A number of internationally recognized films have been made partly or entirely on location in Brazil. One of the most noteworthy

The proliferation of spray-painted graffiti on the buildings and monuments of Rio de Janeiro inspired the city government to provide large chalkboards and chalk for people who want to express themselves in public.

Decorative feather work and beadwork, traditional crafts that have been practiced by the Indians for centuries, are preserved and displayed at this Carnaval parade.

is *Black Orpheus*, a retelling of the ancient Greek myth of Orpheus and Eurydice, with the setting changed to Carnaval. It was filmed in a favela of Rio that has since been torn down. *The Emerald Forest* concerns the kidnapping of a white boy who grows up with an Indian tribe called the Invisible People in the Amazon forest. *The Mission* tells of the Jesuits' work with the Indians in the 18th century and of the conflicts between the Jesuits and the landowners over the treatment of the Indians. The center of action of *Fitzcarraldo* is Peru, but this film includes scenes of the Amazon River and of the opera house at Manaus. Although all of these movies tell fictional tales, their scenic backgrounds are accurate and realistic.

Traditional Art Forms

Before the coming of the Portuguese, Brazil's Indians had developed many traditional art forms. Handsome pottery that included dishes, vases, and burial urns was crafted on the island of Marajo on the Amazon and elsewhere. The Arawaks made dance masks in animal shapes. Decorative feather work, beadwork, and the weaving of baskets, mats, and hammocks were practiced by most tribes. Stonework utensils and jewelry were made in the southern part of Brazil.

One craft that is a legacy from Portugal is lace making. Other crafts with a European flavor are wood carving, the making of folk dolls, leather work, goldsmithing, and the forging and decorating of ornate silver gaucho knives. The black-and-white wave-patterned mosaic sidewalks of Copacabana Beach were modeled after the mosaics of Lisbon, Portugal.

Folklore is a rich form of communication, entertainment, and education in Brazil. Traditional Indian stories concerned animals (especially the jaguar and the anaconda), tricksters, and mythical beings with oddly shaped bodies who lived in the forest or in rivers. A current of humor and earthiness underlies many of these tales. Although the shrinking of the Indian population and the gradual disappearance of the traditional Indian way of life have meant that many aspects of Indian culture are lost forever, scholars and Indians alike have recognized the need to preserve folktales, crafts, and other cultural artifacts. Several institutes have been set up to record and study Indian folklore—in some cases, young people of Indian descent from the cities have studied at these centers in order to discover their Indian heritage.

Women in a Rio favela meet at a common washing area because water, like every other basic necessity, is scarce.

8

The Future of Brazil

Brazil is in many ways a paradox, a place of contradictions. Within sight of luxurious and expensive high-rise apartment towers, people live in shacks without running water or electricity, unable to feed their children. Indians in the Amazon Basin, living as their ancestors did for thousands of years, are threatened by armies of land developers and by the high-technology invasion of highways, oil wells, and hydroelectric dams. At the dawn of the 1990s, many Brazilians express a deepening despair about the future. Hope that everyone will have a chance to lead a decent life seems to be dwindling in Brazil.

Brazil shares many of the widespread problems of the modern world, but its most serious problem is economic. Because Brazil is trying to pay off its huge foreign debt at the same time that inflation drives up prices within the country, little government money is available for social services or other domestic matters, and poverty afflicts half of the population. People abandon children they cannot feed, and crowds loot supermarkets for food. Some Brazilians feel that the foreign debt is being paid in human suffering and that the 1980s have been a decade of hardship.

103

The strength of Brazil lies in its youth: The state of Rio de Janeiro has made an effort to enroll some 300,000 children in new public schools. This one was converted from an abandoned luxury hotel and casino.

One possible solution to the economic problem is for Brazil to turn its back on the world, to become entirely self-sufficient, and to stop payment on the debt. Another is to pay back the debt by putting the money into environmental projects that would benefit the entire world, such as preservation of the rain forest. But Brazil may be too suspicious of the motives of other countries to take such a step. After decades of emphasis on the need to modernize, industrialize, and enter the modern world, Brazil's government is reluctant to heed the urgings of the United States and some European countries to halt development in the Amazon. After all, some Brazilian leaders reason, those nations already possess fully developed industries—why should they hold Brazil back from achieving the same thing?

Brazilians are seeking political solutions to their problems, looking for a leader who can restore a better standard of living. Many of the country's leaders throughout its history have been strong, charismatic, popular personalities who have captured the public's imagination and risen to power on the cheers of the crowds. Many of these patriarchal leaders, however, were either corrupt or incompetent.

Brazil is a country with enormous potential. It has the resources, the labor force, and the vitality to become one of the great nations of the world if its current problems can be overcome. If its economy improves and it manages to achieve a balance between exploiting and preserving its forests and other natural resources, Brazil will continue to lead the developing nations of the Third World well into the 21st century.

GLOSSARY

bandeiras   Literally, "flags." Expeditions led by raiders that extended the boundaries of Brazil.

café com leite   Coffee with milk.

Candomblé   An African-Brazilian religion that combines elements of Catholic, African, and Indian beliefs.

capoeira   An acrobatic, dancelike form of foot fighting that has West African roots.

carioca   A resident of Rio de Janeiro.

Carnaval   The exuberant festival of music, parades, costumes, and parties that precedes Lent.

conversos   Jews who were forcibly converted to Christianity in Spain and Portugal during the 1500s and 1600s.

degredados   Portuguese criminals who were set ashore in Brazil to learn the Indians' languages and to convert them, if possible, to Christianity.

favelado   The resident of a favela.

favelas   Squatter settlements in Rio and other cities.

fazenda   A large estate of agricultural land.

feijoada   The Brazilian national dish, a stew of meat and black beans.

gaucho   A cowboy of the south of Brazil.

mandioca   Also known as cassava or manioc. A root
native to Brazil; when processed it yields a
flour that is used in breads, puddings, stews,
and soup. Tapioca is made from the plant.

maté   A tea from the dried leaves of an evergreen tree;
it is made into a beverage called *chimarrão*.

Papai Noel   Father Christmas.

paulista   A resident of São Paulo.

samba   A distinctive Brazilian music and dance that
flourishes during Carnaval.

sertão   The interior of the country, particularly in the
northeast.

INDEX

A

Abreu, Casimiro de, 94
Acre (state), 18, 27
Africa, 15, 19, 29, 42, 47, 51, 52
African-Brazilian spiritism, 55–56, 70
Agriculture, 19, 28, 65, 85–87
Almeida Neves, Tancredo de, 49
Amado, Jorge, 94
Amaral, Tarsila do, 96–97
Amazonas (state), 18
Amazon Basin, 21, 22, 90, 103
Amazonia region, 18, 22, 85, 104
Amazon River, 21, 25–26, 52, 85
Andes Mountains, 25, 90
Andrade, Carlos Drummond de, 94
Animals, 24–25, 30
Architecture, 97
Argentina, 21, 44
Art, 96–97
Asia, 19, 47, 53
Atlantic Ocean, 21, 22, 25

B

Bahia, 29, 42, 52, 56, 66, 67, 94
Bandeira, Manuel, 94
Bandeirantes, 41–42, 43
Belém, 25, 98
Belo Horizonte, 84
Bolivia, 21

Bonaparte, Napoleon, 44
Braga, Sonia, 99
Brasília, 28, 29, 47–48, 49, 73, 91
Brazil,
   customs, 67–69
   economy, 47, 83–84, 88–89, 103–4
   elections, 49
   employment, 65–66
   future, 103–5
   gender roles, 68–69
   independence of, 43–45
   origin of "Brazil," 38–39
   people, 51–54
   quality of life, 56, 65
   size, 15, 21
   traditional art forms, 101
   urban problems, 32

C

Cabral, Pedro Álvares, 38
Calvalcanti, Emiliano di, 96
Canada, 21
Cape Verde Islands, 38
Carnaval, 32, 67, 69, 71, 87, 98
Chile, 21, 90
China, 21
Christ the Redeemer statue, 31
Climate, 28–29, 31–32, 34
Clothing, 66–67
Collor de Mello, Fernando, 13, 49

Colombia, 21, 22, 41
Constitution, 46, 49, 74–75
Corcovado Mountain, 31
Costa, Lúcio, 97
Cruzado Plan, 49
Cuisine, 66
Cunha, Euclides da, 93
Currency, 88

D

Diamantina, 43
Dias Gomes, Alfredo, 95
Dutch, 42

E

Ecuador, 21
Education, 78–80

F

Favelas, 16, 32, 56
Fishing, 26, 87
Foreign aid, 88
Fortaleza, 28
France, 42, 44
Freire, Paulo, 95
French Guiana, 21

G

Gauchos, 34, 67
Geography, 15, 21–35
Georgi, Bruno, 97
Germany, 46, 47, 53
Gomes, Antonio Carlos, 98
Government, 16, 73–74
Great Escarpment, 22
Guanabara Bay, 39
Guiana Highlands, 22
Guyana, 21

H

Health care, 80–81
Henry the Navigator, prince of
  Portugal, 38
History, 37–49
  early explorers, 38–39
  early settlers, 39
  modern history, 46–49
Holidays, 69–71
Homeless children. *See* Brazil,
  urban problems
Human rights, 77–78

I

Iberian Peninsula, 38
Iemanjá, 70
Iguaçú Falls, 35
Industry, 19
Instituto Butantan, 33
Ipiuranga River, 44
Itaipu Dam, 34–35
Italy, 47, 53

J

Japan, 53
Jesuits, 42, 98, 100
John VI, king of Portugal, 44

K

Kaiapos, 52
Kubitschek de Oliveira, Juscelino,
  47

L

Language, 15, 56
Le Corbusier, 97
Libraries, 98

Lisboa, Antônio Francisco, 96
Lispector, Clarice, 94
Literature, 93–95

M

Mabe, Manabu, 96
Machado de Assis, Joaquim Maria, 93
Manufacturing, 65, 84
Maracanã Stadium, 32
Marx, Roberto Burle, 97
Media, 91
Meireles, Cecília, 94
Mello Freyre, Gilberto de, 94
Melo Neto, João Cabral de, 94, 95
Mendes, Francisco "Chico", 27
Mexico City, Mexico, 32
Military, 48–49, 76
Minas Gerais, 43
Mining, 43, 65, 84–85
Miranda, Carmen, 99
Morais, Vinícius de, 94
Movies, 98–100
Museums, 97–98
Music, 98

N

Native American Indians, 15, 37–38, 40, 42, 51–52, 98, 100, 103
New York City, 16
Niemeyer, Oscar, 48, 97
Nile River, 25
Northeast region, 28–29

P

Palace of Culture, 97
Palmares, 42
Pantanal, 29–30

Paraguay, 21, 34
Paraná, 46
Paraná River, 35
Paul Afonso Falls, 28
Pedro I, Emperor of Brazil, 44
Pedro II, Emperor of Portugal, 44–45
Pelé, 71
Peru, 21, 25, 41, 89
Pico da Neblina, 22
Piranhas, 26
Plants, 22–23
Poland, 53
Police force, 77
Political parties, 75–76
Population, 19
Portinari, Cândido, 97
Portugal, 15, 16, 37, 38–40, 42, 43, 44, 51, 53, 85
Poverty, 16, 32
Prevsaude, 81

Q

Queirós, Rachel de, 94

R

Rain forests, 17–18, 22–28
Recife, 28, 94
Recreation, 71
Rêgo, José Lins do, 94
Religion, 15, 54–56
Resources, 83
Ribeiro, João Ubaldo, 94
Rio de Janeiro, 16, 31, 39, 44, 56, 69, 77, 81, 84, 85, 87, 88, 90, 91, 97, 98
Roman Catholicism, 15, 55
Rondônia (state), 18
Rosa, João Guimãraes, 94

Rubber tapping, 26–27
Rubião, Murilo, 94

S

Salvador, 28
Samba music, 71
Sambodromo, 32, 69
Santos, 34, 90
São Francisco River, 28, 39
São Paulo, 16, 31–34, 40, 42, 49, 69,
  81, 84, 90, 91, 96, 97, 98
São Vicente, 40
Sarney, José, 49, 75–76, 89
Segall, Lasar, 96
Slavery, 40–42, 45, 52
South Africa, 43
South America, 15, 16, 19, 21, 32, 42
Southeast region, 31–34
Souza, Marcio, 94
Soviet Union, 21
Spain, 38, 40, 42, 53
Sports, 71
Suassuna, Ariano, 95
Sugarloaf Mountain, 31
Sugar plantations, 43
Suriname, 21

T

Tiradentes (Joaquim José da Silva
  Xavier), 43–44, 69

Tordesillas, Treaty of, 38, 43
Tourism, 87
Trade, 87
Transportation, 89–91

U

United States, 16, 19, 21, 43, 44,
  46, 47, 87, 104
Urucu, 85
Uruguay, 21

V

Vargas, Getúlio, 47
Venezuela, 21, 22
Vespucci, Amerigo, 39
Villa-Lobos, Heitor, 98
Voting, 77

W

West central region, 29–31
World War I, 46–47
World War II, 19, 47, 76

X

Xingu River, 52

Z

Zumbi, 42